Credits

Animals in Time—Vol 1: Historical Empires and Civilizations
Copyright © 2018 by Hosanna Rodriguez

ISBN 978-0-9963258-3-7

Front cover art by McKenna Keefer

Cover graphics by Genesis Moss Keefer
www.genesismoss.com

Proofread by Traci Post

Animals in Time, Volume 1 Activity Book was created by:

LET'S LEARN, KIDS!

www.letslearnkids.com

This activity book accompanies the Animals in Time, Volume 1 storybook comprised of twenty-six A-Z animal adventure stories. These activities will engage your child in the various topics introduced in the stories, which include history, animals, geography, science, and a whole lot of fun! This resource is ideal for elementary students and can be combined with a letter of the week approach.

The following activities are based on each story:

- coloring pages
- history/civilization activities
- animal facts with mazes and art
- tell me about the animal
- science activities
- geography mapping
- notebook pages for child's own writing (fiction or nonfiction)

The classroom tools below can be found at LetsLearnKids.com, under the Animals in Time dropdown menu. The classroom tools include:

- 26 lesson plans, including group games and snack ideas
- class sign-in sheet template
- animal habitat train graphics

As with the Animals in Time storybook, this project provided young people the opportunity to further develop a wide variety of skills, including artistic expression, research, writing, publishing tactics, and more, while transforming their passions into something that is valuable for others.

Our hope is that your child will enjoy their adventures with the Animals, and that they too will be inspired to create as they engage with what they're learning!

TABLE OF CONTENTS

YANNI THE YAK

Y1 Coloring page

Y2 History/Civilization: What Time is it?

Y3 Yak facts, maze, art

Y4 Tell Me About Yaks

Y5 Science: Caught in an Oasis

   Geography: Oceans

Y6 Notebook page

ZERLOCK THE ZEBRA

Z1 Coloring page

Z2 History/Civilization: Find Each Freedom Seeker

Z3 Zebra facts, maze, art

Z4 Tell Me About Zebras

Z5 Science: No Ordinary Stone

   Geography: Continents

Z6 Notebook page

AMBER THE ANT

SOLVE THE TABLET MYSTERY!

The Ten Commandments were not originally written in modern Hebrew. Different stages of the Hebrew language, like other ancient languages, did not contain vowels in written form.

Just for fun, try solving the code shown on this tablet. Use the vowel key below.

Vowel Key

▷ = A
◈ = E
✹ = I
✖ = O
● = U
☆ = Y

Write the message here:

____

____

____

____

____

____

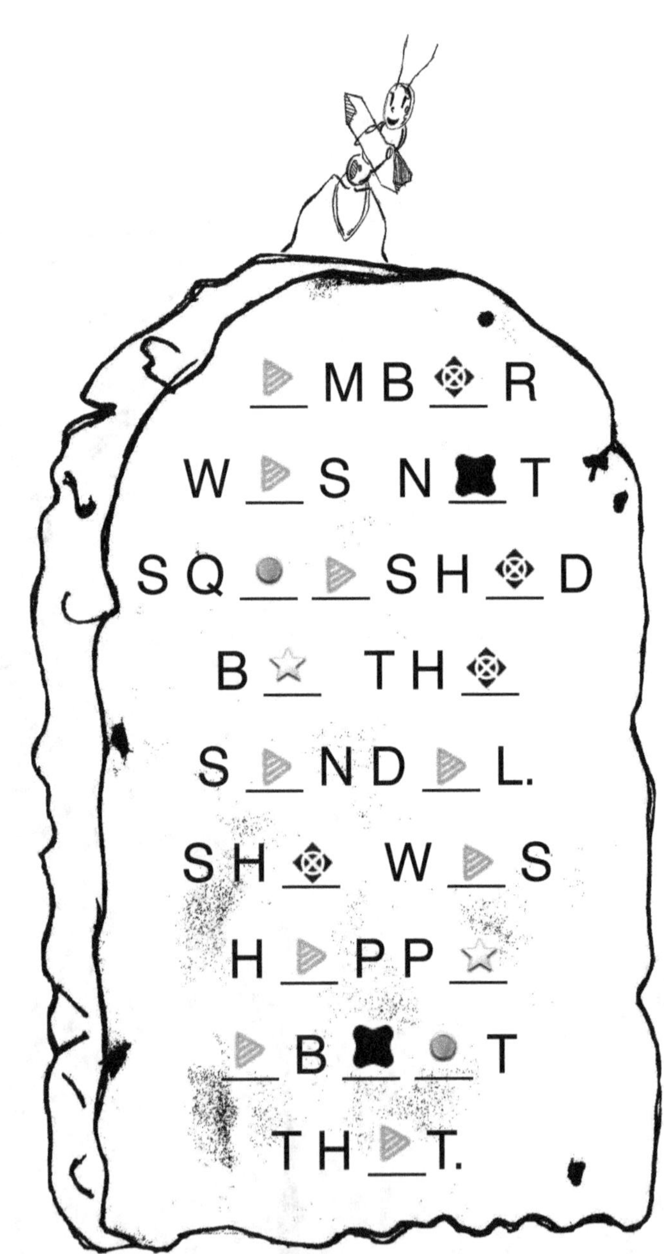

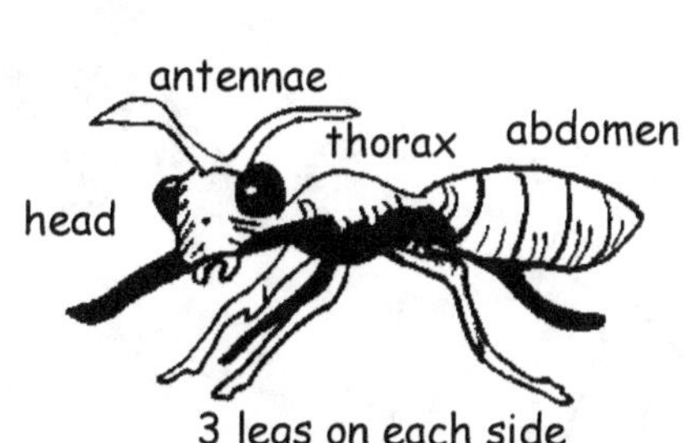

ANTS

Ants are insects that live in communities, or colonies, and the members of the community depend on one another.

The ant has a typical insect body, which has three main parts: the head, thorax, and abdomen. Its skeleton is on the outside of its body, and it's called an exoskeleton. They have two antennae and six legs. There are four stages of an ant's life cycle: egg, larva, pupa, and adult.

Ants are found in nearly every kind of habitat, except where it is really cold. Most ant species build underground nests made up of tunnels and chambers, or rooms, for food storage, nurseries, resting (because ants get tired after all that work!), and the queen.

Depending on the type of ant, the foods they eat can include plants, pollen, other insects, animals, and everything in your picnic basket!

There are many dangers for ants, including anteaters, frogs, lizards, spiders, and the bottom of your shoe!

Help Amber find her way through the ant hill. She is on her way to a summer music festival.

Draw your own ant nest. Include rooms for food storage, babies, and more.

Tell me about . . .

ANTS

A4

What do I eat?

What am I scared of?

What else do you know about me?

Try to draw me!

LEGOS AND LIVING THINGS

Have you ever played with Legos? Have you ever sorted them, putting them into groups, so you can find what you need to build your next great Lego creation? Let's say your Legos only come in three colors–blue, red, and yellow. You might group all the blue together in one pile, and then do the same with the other colors. Now, with the blue pile, you separate all the blue building blocks from the blue Lego men helmets and clear blue blocks (good for water scenes). Then, with the blue building blocks, you separate them by size, and so on. What have you done? You have just classified your Legos!

Well, there is also a way to classify all living things on this planet, and we give the classifications, or groups, their own names: domain, kingdom, phylum, class, order, family, genus, and species. A simple way to remember them is using the saying "ducks keep ponds clean or frogs get sick."

Here are two steps to help you remember the names of the groups of living things:

1. Draw a line from the A column to the B column to find the correct order. *Hint: match the first letters of each word in the columns.*

2. Write each of the group names from column B in the correct order on the numbered lines.

▶ The first one has been done for you!

A	B
1. Ducks	Phylum
2. Keep	Class
3. Ponds	Domain
4. Clean	Order
5. Or	Kingdom
6. Frogs	Species
7. Get	Genus
8. Sick	Family

1. _Domain_
2. ____________
3. ____________
4. ____________
5. ____________
6. ____________
7. ____________
8. ____________

FERTILE CRESCENT

MAP IT!

Scout ants searched far and wide for their leader. Color the items listed below on the map.

1. Color the Mediterranean Sea BLUE.

2. Color the Tigris River BLUE.

3. Color the Euphrates River BLUE.

4. Circle Mesopotamia in RED.

5. Circle Sumer in ORANGE.

A6

BAREND THE BEAR

FOLLOW THE FOOTSTEPS UP MOUNT SINAI

Amber the Ant and Barend the Bear spent time on Mount Sinai looking for food. It was on this rocky peak that they discovered the pair of sandal-covered feet belonging to the one who carried the tablets with the Ten Commandments.

Here's your challenge:

Figure out how many feet Mount Sinai stands by counting each footstep. Once you count them all, multiply that number by 100, and you will have the answer. Write the answer here ___________.

Tips:
If you know how to count by 2s, you will count the footsteps faster!
Ask someone older to multiply the answer by 100 if you need help.

BEARS

Bears are mammals: they have hair and a spine. They feed their babies milk and are warm-blooded. They also live on nearly all continents except Antarctica and Australia.

Bears are big animals. They can swim and climb trees. And they are clever too. There is not much they are afraid of. If they have cubs, though, watch out! Mama bears are very protective of their babies.

Bears like to eat! They are omnivores and eat meat, plants, and anything left behind by campers. They have a reputation for loving honey, and boy, do they love it! They can eat practically all day and night, especially as winter approaches, when they find a safe and comfortable spot to sleep throughout winter. This is called hibernation. A mother bear will enter her den when she is expecting a cub, which means it is still growing inside her. Sometimes she may be expecting two or three cubs. Buy the time spring arrives, she leaves the den with a baby cub—or two or three.

Cubs live with their mothers for about three years, and then they are ready to face life on their own.

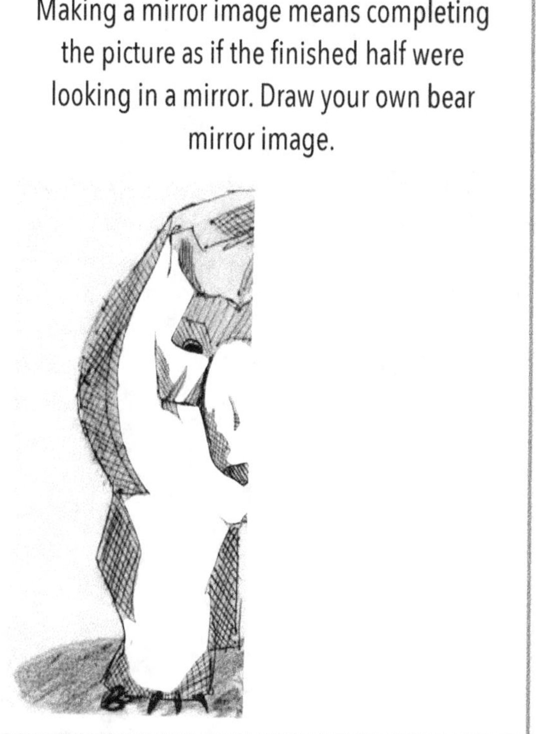

Making a mirror image means completing the picture as if the finished half were looking in a mirror. Draw your own bear mirror image.

BEARS

B4

What do I eat?

What do I like to do during the day?

What else do you know about me?

Try to draw me or my footprint (paw print)!

KINGDOM DELIVERIES

B5

Living things come in all shapes in sizes. You know that you are alive. You know that all people and animals are alive. But there is so much more living on this planet besides only people and animals. Remember how living things are classified (or grouped)? Well, the first step in classifying living things is to group them together into six kingdoms.

Some examples from the six kingdoms:

Animalia–birds, mammals, insects, reptiles, and amphibians

Plantae–plants that make their own food to survive; flowering plants, mosses, and ferns

Fungi–look like plants but don't make their own food and live on decaying organisms; mushrooms and yeasts

Protista–one-celled organisms; slime molds, giant kelp seaweed

Archaea–live in extreme conditions; thermophiles in very hot geysers

Bacteria–one-celled organisms; some are good like the ones in yogurt, and some are bad like *E.coli*

The horses are bringing bundles to the kingdoms of living things. Draw a line from each kingdom's castle to the correct bundle of living things.

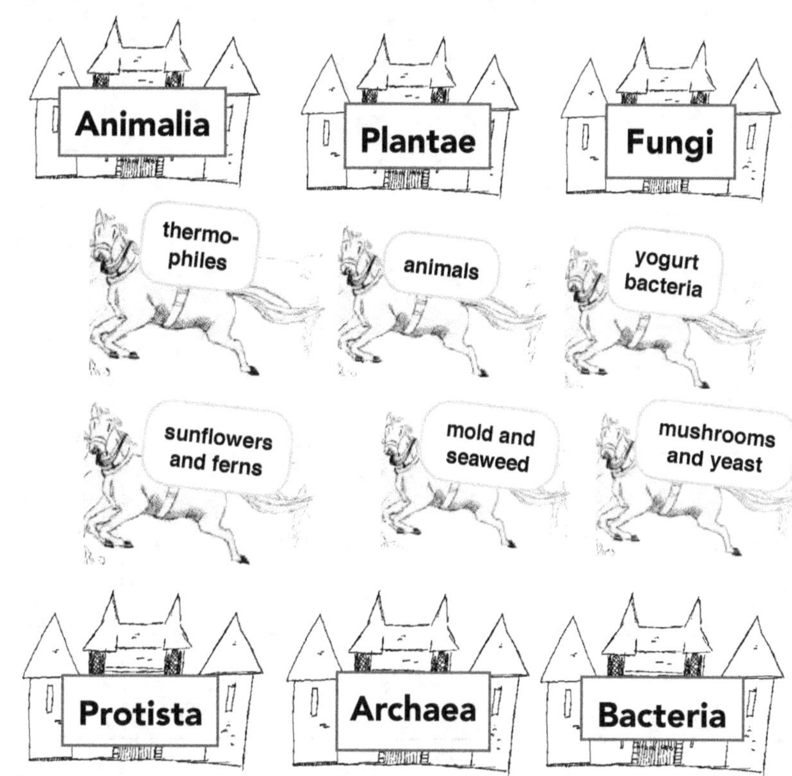

ASSYRIAN EMPIRE

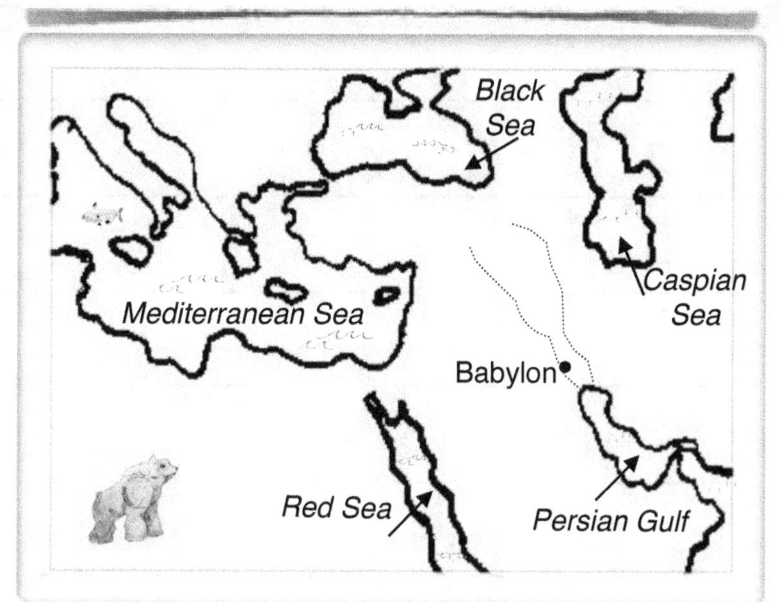

MAP IT!

Barend the Bear traveled to the locations below. Color the following items on the map.

1. Color the Black Sea BLACK.

2. Color the Caspian Sea GREEN.

3. Color the Red Sea RED.

4. Color the Persian Gulf BLUE.

5. Circle Babylon in ORANGE.

CORA THE CATERPILLAR

FIND THE CATERPILLAR AMONG THE GODS

The Greeks and Romans had different names for the same gods. Search for Cora on each of the gods, and circle her.

C2

ZEUS / JUPITER

HERA / JUNO

ATHENA / MINERVA

HERMES / MERCURY

APHRODITE / VENUS

ARES / MARS

POSEIDON / NEPTUNE

www.letslearnkids.com

© 2018 Hosanna Rodriguez

CATERPILLARS

Caterpillars are insects. They have two antennae on their heads and eight pairs of legs. Sixteen legs are a lot of legs!

Caterpillars turn into either butterflies or moths. When these creatures are two to four weeks old, they begin making a chrysalis, or cocoon. A butterfly makes a chrysalis, and a moth makes a cocoon. There are four stages of a caterpillar's life cycle: egg, larva (caterpillar stage), pupa (chrysalis stage), and adult (butterfly or moth stage).

Caterpillars don't breathe through their mouths—they breathe through little holes on the sides of their bodies called spiracles. This is good because their mouths are always busy chewing, chewing, chewing! Most caterpillars are herbivores, which means they only eat plants such as leaves and fruit. There are some, however, that eat other insects or insect eggs.

Predators of caterpillars include wasps, birds, and some mammals. Baby Old World Swallowtail caterpillars look like bird droppings, which is a good camouflage.

Butterflies often lay their eggs under leaves. Draw a caterpillar that has just emerged from its egg, hanging upside-down.

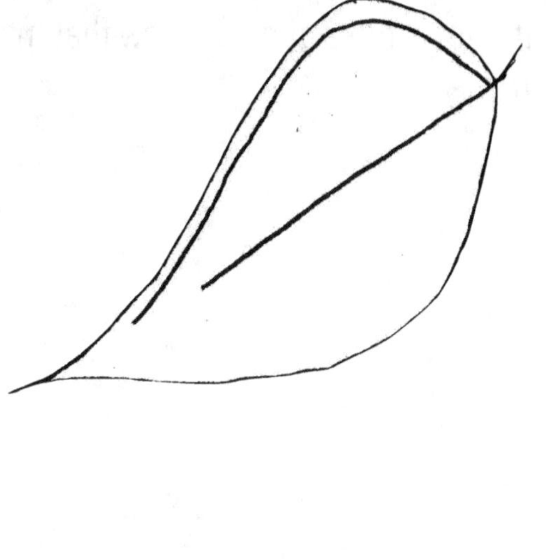

CATERPILLARS

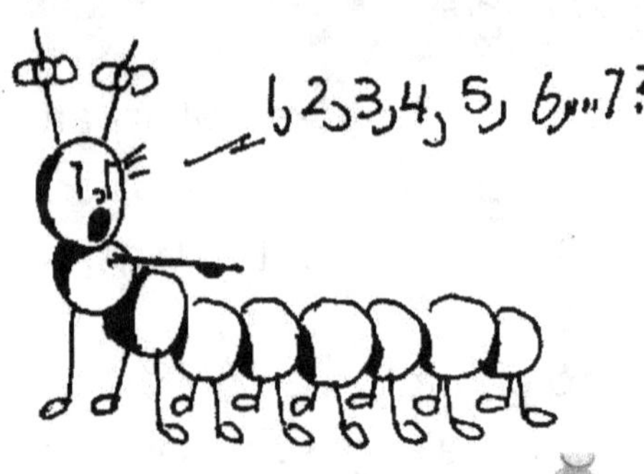

What do I eat?

What eats me?

How many legs do I really have (not shown in the pictures above)? Draw that many legs below.

There are 4 stages in my growth, from egg to butterfly. Try to draw the stages in my life cycle below.

EXPLORE AN ANIMAL CELL

Cells are the building blocks in all living things. Since we've already started talking about Legos… Imagine a finished Lego creation is a living thing, and the individual blocks are its cells. Well, every living thing is made up of cells, and all cells have parts inside that help it function.

Here are some of the parts in an animal's cell:

Nucleus–the brain of the cell; it directs the cell's activities

Cytoplasm–holds all the parts in place

Vacuole–a storage container for food or waste, or anything else it needs or wants to keep separate from the rest

Mitochondria–the energy-maker

Cell membrane–the cell wall; it protects the cell

Golgi bodies–flat like a stack of pancakes; in charge of packaging and shipping off proteins

Imagine Cora the Caterpillar shrunk down to an itty-bitty size and wanted to take a trip through an animal cell, ending at the nucleus. Draw a line of her path as she travels from the cell membrane, to the Golgi bodies, to the mitochondria, to the cytoplasm, to the vacuole, and finally to the nucleus!

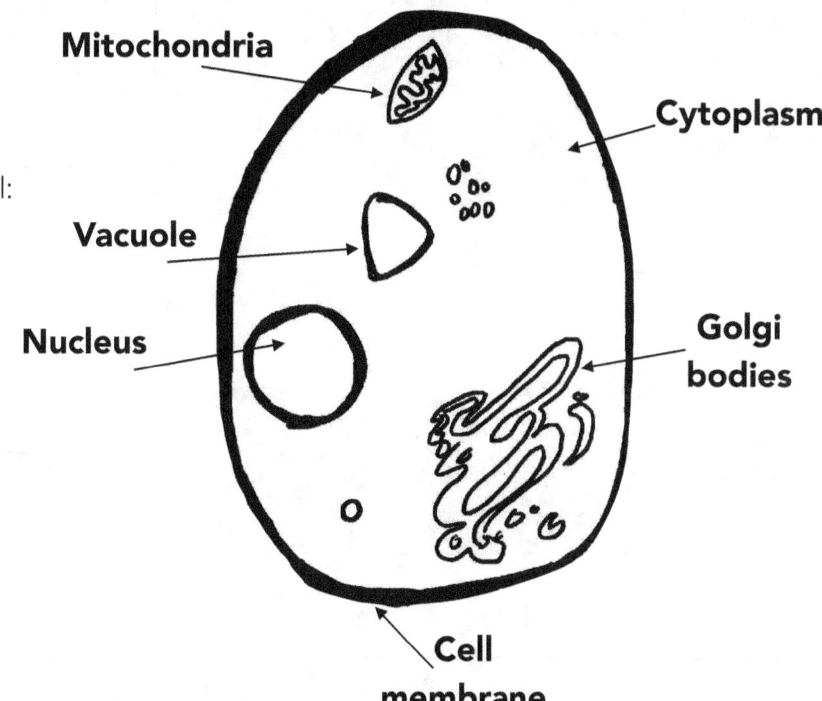

HEBREW EMPIRE

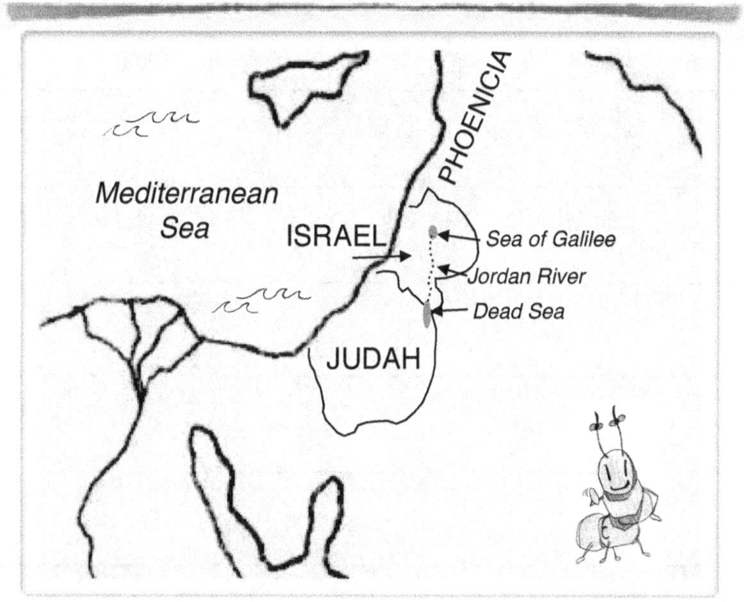

MAP IT!

Cora and her friends found a map during their trip to Greece. Color the items below on the map.

1. Circle Phoenicia in RED.

2. Color the Sea of Galilee GREEN.

3. Color the Jordan River BLUE.

4. Color the Dead Sea PURPLE.

5. Color Israel YELLOW.

6. Color Judah ORANGE.

DANIEL THE DUCK

THE SEVEN WONDERS OF THE ANCIENT WORLD

Daniel the Duck enjoyed living on the Lighthouse at Alexandria, with the Pyramids of Giza nearby. He wanted to visit the other wonders of the ancient world, though. Where do you think he'd most want to go? On the lines below the names, number the locations in the order that YOU think he would have chosen. His lighthouse has already been numbered—1, of course.

PHAROS LIGHTHOUSE
AT ALEXANDRIA
AND PYRAMIDS OF
GIZA

__1__

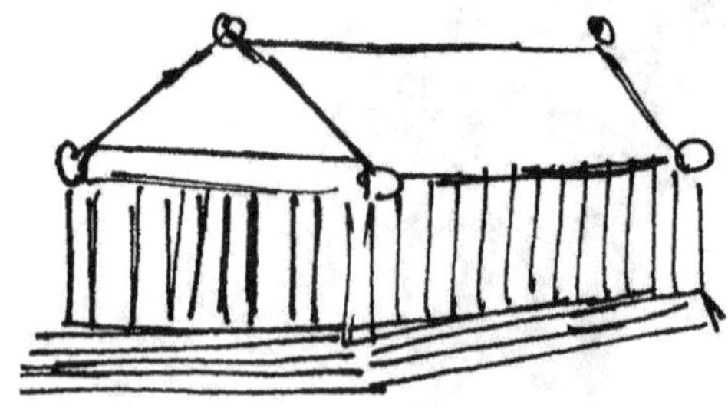

TEMPLE OF ARTEMIS
AT EPHESUS

_____

MAUSOLEUM AT
HALICARNASSUS

_____

COLOSSUS OF RHODES

_____

HANGING GARDENS OF BABYLON

_____

STATUE OF ZEUS AT OLYMPIA

_____

DUCKS

patterns in
their feathers

webbed feet

Ducks are little birds that live on the water. They are very good swimmers, and they have special oil on their feathers to help them slide through the water. Harlequin ducks, like Daniel, have colorful patterns on their heads that make them look like they came out of a circus!

The mommy duck builds her nest under or behind bushes and rocks near the water. She makes the nest out of grass and twigs, and some of her soft feathers. The mommy then lays around six creamy white eggs, which hatch into ducklings. The babies can swim and dive right away, and they feed themselves with bugs in the water. Adult harlequin ducks eat mainly mussels, crabs, and other things with shells, and sometimes plants.

These ducks dive deep down in the sea, prying mussels off rocks with their sharp beaks. Ouch! Don't let them poke you! Ducks are usually hunted by cats, dogs, hawks, snakes, raccoons, and sometimes angry guards with spears! Look out, Daniel!

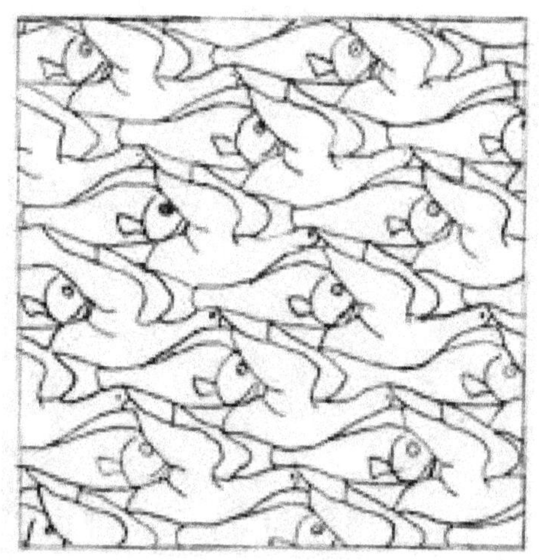

Abstract art doesn't have to look realistic. Using the shapes of ducks and fish, for example, all the spaces are filled in this picture. Now add some color!

DUCKS

D4

What do I eat?

Where do I live?

What am I scared of?

What do I like to do?

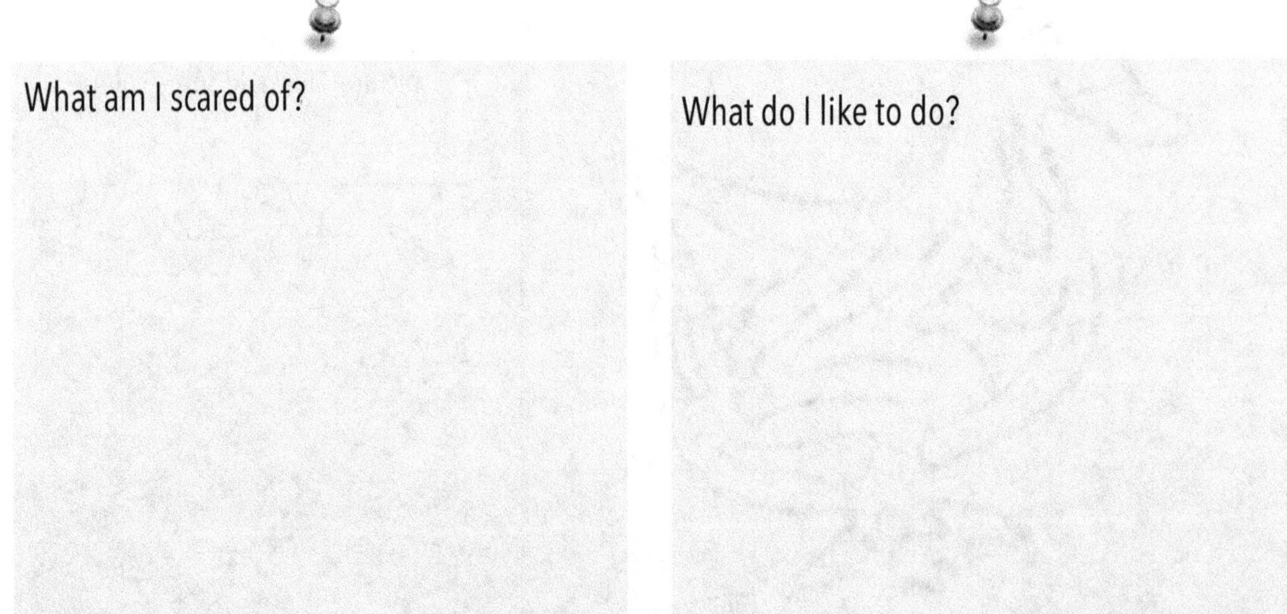

© 2018 Hosanna Rodriguez

WHAT'S IN DANIEL'S TUMMY?

Daniel mostly likes to eat small sea creatures, but he sometimes eats plants. The last time we learned about cells, it was about animal cells. Now let's take a look at plant cells. There are many things that are similar about the two, but there are some differences. Plant cells have a thicker covering, called a cell wall. These cells also have chloroplasts, which absorb sunlight and, along with water and air, make food for the plant.

Try to draw a plant cell.

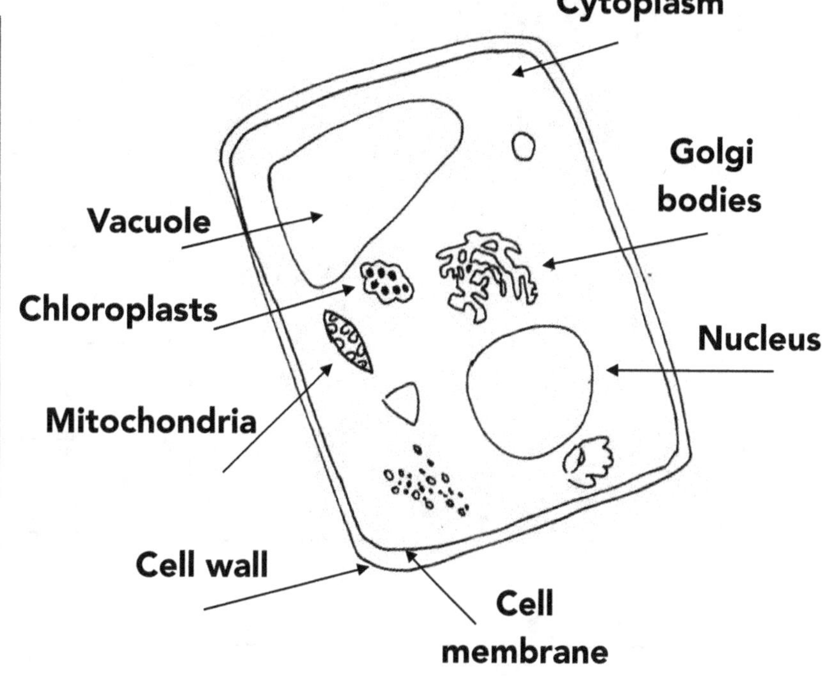

HITTITE EMPIRE

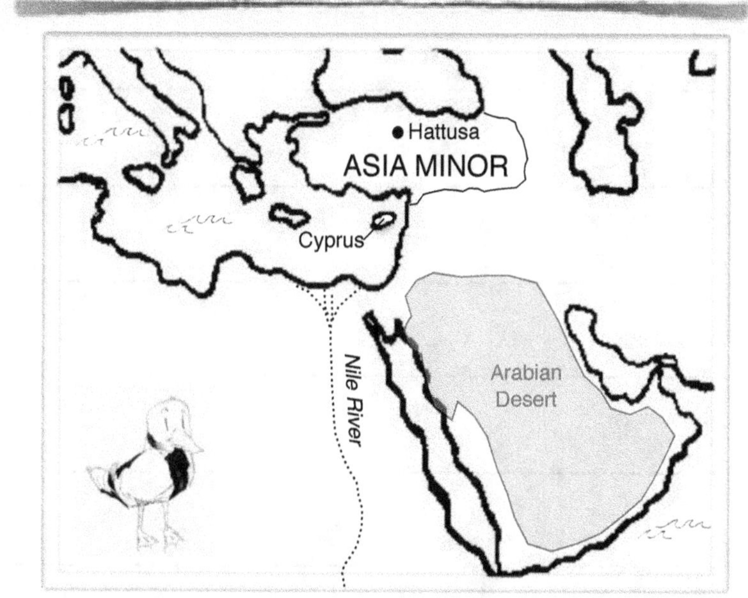

MAP IT!

While trying to find his way back home, Daniel the Duck found a map in a fishing boat. Color what he saw.

1. Circle Hattusa in RED.

2. Color Asia Minor YELLOW.

3. Color Cyprus PINK.

4. Color the Arabian Desert TAN (or BROWN).

ELLA THE EAGLE

COUNT THE ROMAN ARCHES

The building below may look like a birthday cake, but it is one of the great structures from ancient Rome that still stands today. It is called the Roman Colosseum, and the construction was completed in AD 80. This was the time when the Roman Empire ruled. Two hundred years later, the empire was divided into western and eastern empires. And about two hundred years after that, in AD 476, the western empire was attacked and conquered by a Germanic prince called Odovacar.

The Colosseum was used for fighting between Roman gladiators, who were usually slaves, prisoners of war, or criminals. The building could seat 55,000 people, and it had many arched entrances so the spectators could enter and exit easily.

Here's your challenge:
Find out how many arched entrances the Colosseum had by counting the number of eagles stationed below. Next, multiply that number by 10, and you will have your answer!

___ x 10 = ___ arched entrances

THE ROMAN COLOSSEUM

EAGLES

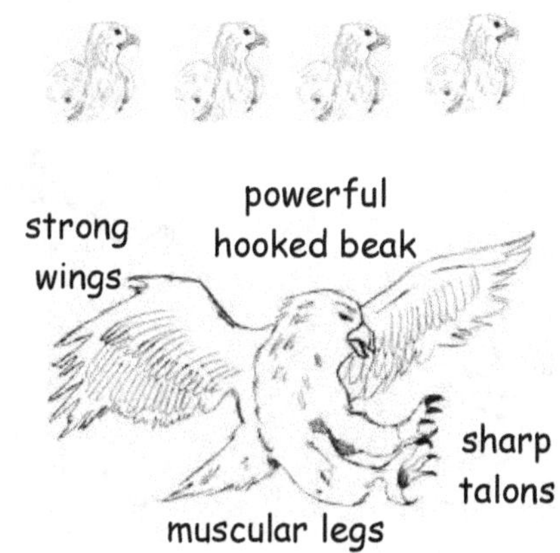

Eagles are large, fierce, and beautiful birds. Ella is a golden eagle, one of the sixty different kinds of eagles in the world! These eagles are much more aggressive and fierce than other kinds.

Eagles are very protective of their territory. To defend their nests, eggs, and young, they make huge loops, dives, and twirls in the sky, scaring off the others. And they're not afraid of soldiers!

As predators, eagles find other animals for food. They hunt using their amazing eyesight, sharp talons, and curving beaks. When the mommy eagle takes care of her eggs, usually two, the daddy goes off to hunt for food for his family, bringing it back to the nest on a cliff or in a tall tree. When the eaglets, or eagle babies, are older, the adults both go off to hunt, working together. Small mammals and birds, like jackrabbits, grouse, and even snakes had better watch out, because they are the main food of the golden eagle.

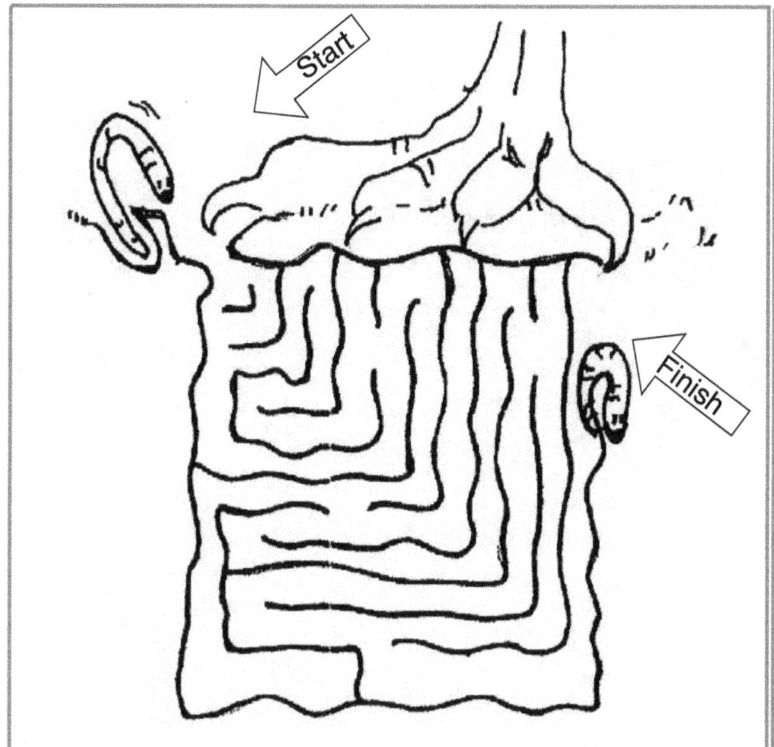

Perspective is important in art because it provides the viewer a specific position from which they see the image. Draw an eagle from the perspective of a creature on the ground.

EAGLES

E4

What do I eat?

Describe my personality. Am I bashful?

What else do you know about me?

Try to draw me!

AN INVERTEBRATE FEAST

E5

Invertebrates are everywhere! They are animals without backbones or bony skeletons, and there are many more of them than backboned creatures.

Some of the major groups of invertebrates are:
Flatworms–usually parasites, living in the body of another creature; have flattened bodies
Roundworms–also parasites, but with round bodies
Segmented worms–known as earthworms; have bodies that are divided into little segments, like rings joined together
Mollusks– soft, squishy creatures like snails, slugs, and octopuses
Sponges–do not have blood or organs; absorb their nutrients from the water
Stinging-cell animals–include organisms like jellyfish, coral, and sea anemones, which all have cells that sting
Sea stars–have spiny skin, suckers, and usually five arms
Arthropods–include insects, spiders, and crustaceans

Ella the Eagle would enjoy a meal of invertebrates. Serve her a meal of the creatures below that you think she would like by drawing them on the plate beneath.

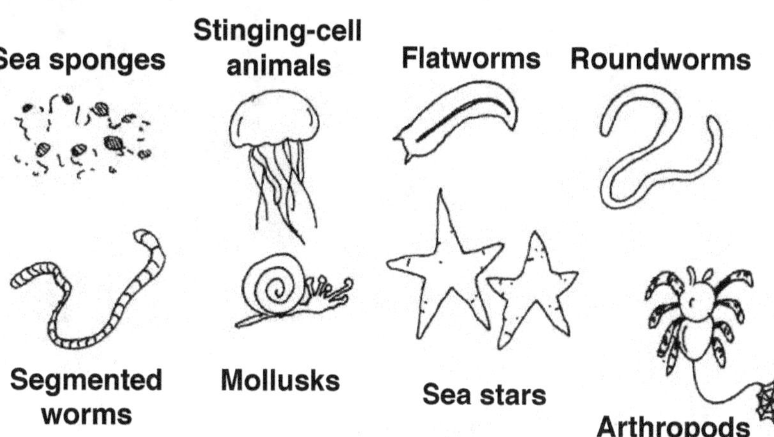

EGYPTIAN EMPIRE

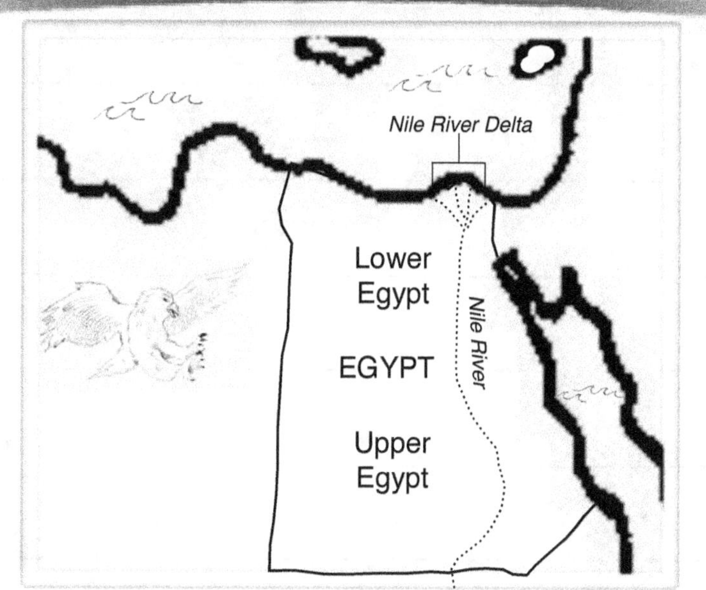

MAP IT!

Ella wasn't about to fall prey to the Visigoths. She was a bird who had been around and knew a thing or two. Color some of the places she had been to.

1. Circle the Nile River Delta in GREEN.

2. Color the Nile River BLUE.

3. Color Lower Egypt YELLOW.

4. Color Upper Egypt ORANGE.

5. Outline Egypt in RED.

E6

FERNANDO THE FROG

GREECE IS FAMOUS

Would you like to live in a country where one person rules, and everyone has to obey, even if the leader has awful ideas? Most people would say no. Well, there is a way for a country to involve the people in which rules are made, and it's called democracy.

Greece is known for developing some of the first democracies long ago, which has inspired other countries to do the same. There were also some people from Greece who further developed the areas of writing, such as Homer, a poet; math, such as Pythagoras, a mathematician; in ideas, such as Socrates, a philosopher; and engineering, such as Archimedes, an inventor.

What about you?

Are you a person who likes to write, work with numbers and shapes, think about many things in life, or invent things? Write the name of one or more of these Greek creators you think you're most like:

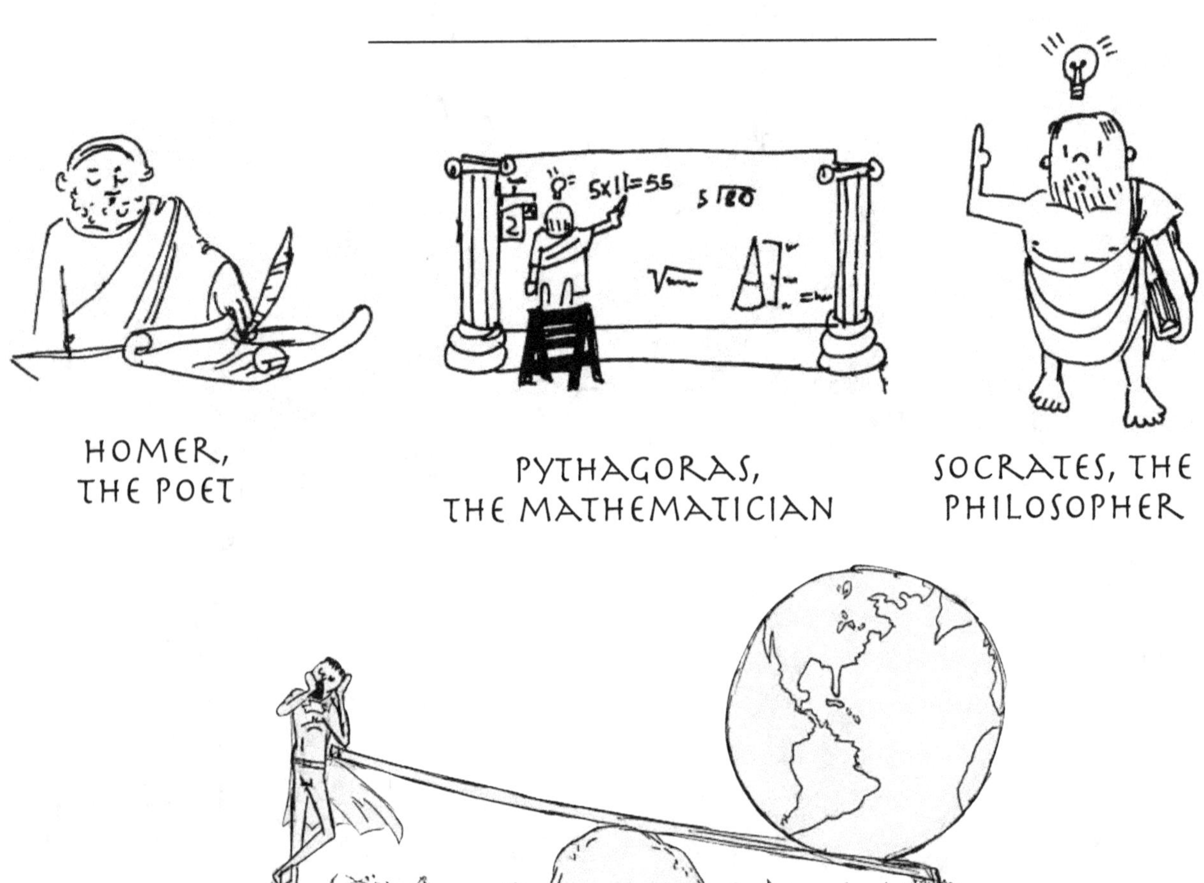

HOMER,
THE POET

PYTHAGORAS,
THE MATHEMATICIAN

SOCRATES, THE
PHILOSOPHER

ARCHIMEDES,
THE INVENTOR

FROGS

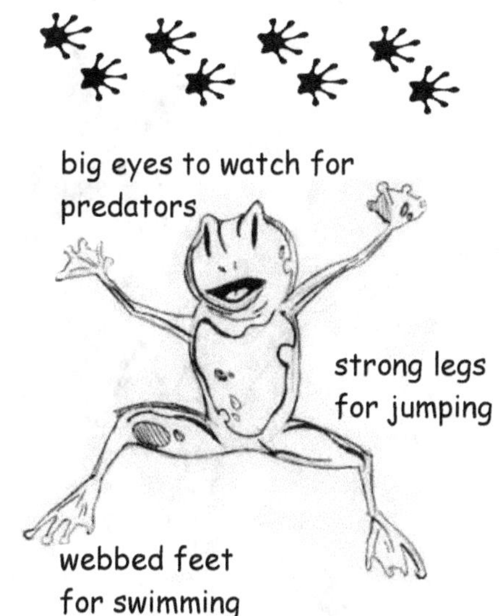

Fernando is a Mediterranean tree frog. He has brownish golden eyes, a dark face stripe, and a white belly. As an amphibian, he has long arms and legs and sticky fingers for climbing. Unlike the similar common tree frog, a Mediterranean tree frog is bluish green and has a thinner body.

Frogs are amazing amphibians. They breathe and drink through their skin, swallow using their eyes, and can see almost all the way around without having to move their heads! They can also hibernate or enter torpor if it gets too hot, too cold, or too dry. A group of frogs is called an army. Look out! Here they come!

Mediterranean tree frogs are good swimmers, and they live near fresh water in trees and grasses. They lay a lot of eggs; sometimes a thousand! They eat insects like beetles and butterflies, but they have to look out for larger animals and birds that might eat them. No wonder Fernando was a little worried when Barend and Ella came up to him!

Draw a couple of frog prints.

Tell me about . . .

FROGS

F4

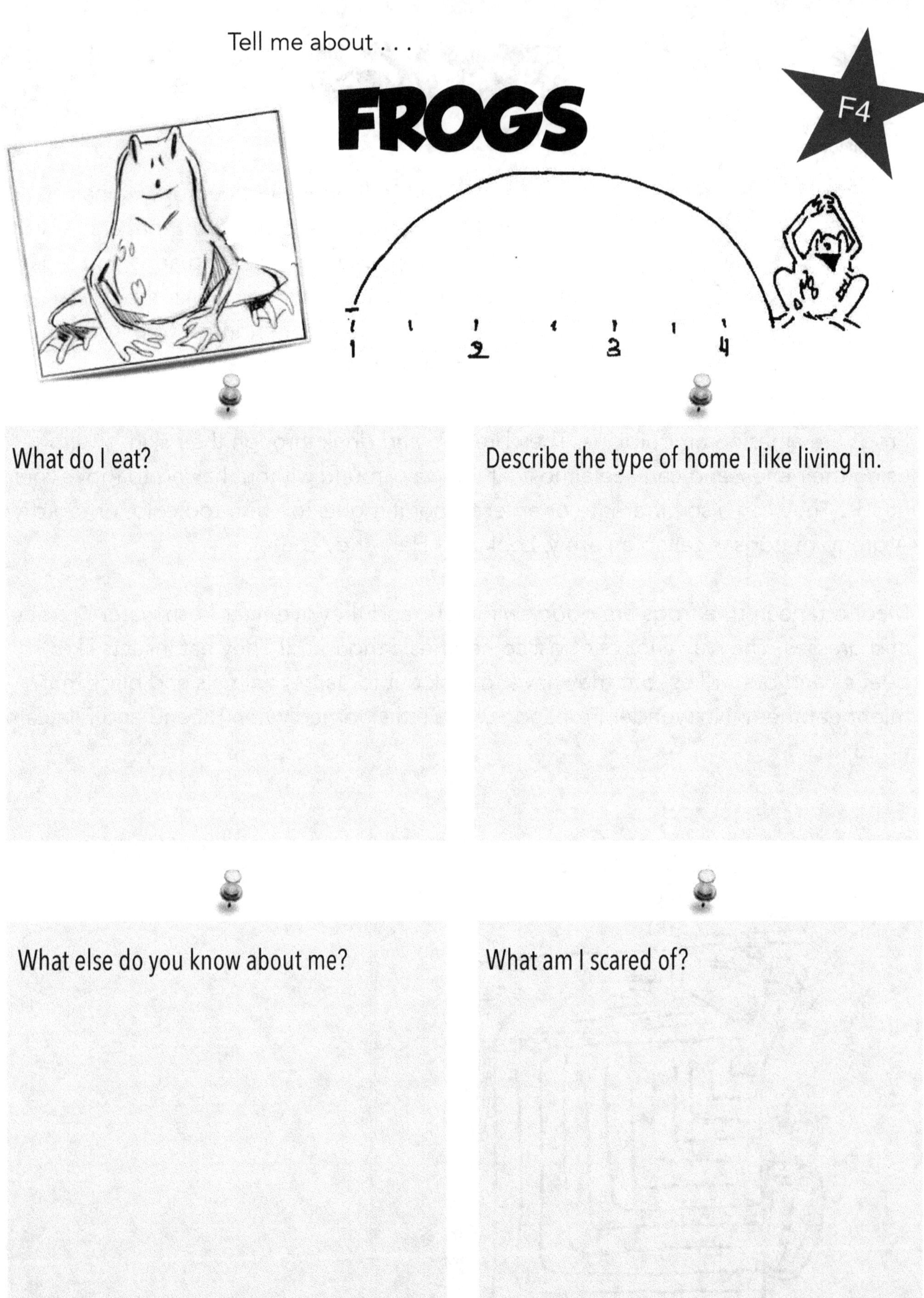

What do I eat?

Describe the type of home I like living in.

What else do you know about me?

What am I scared of?

MATCH THE VERTEBRATES

Vertebrates are animals that have backbones, and that includes fish, birds, amphibians, reptiles, and mammals.

Some of the major groups of vertebrates are:

Fish–live in the water, have gills and fins, and are cold-blooded

Birds–lay eggs and have feathers, wings, and a beak

Amphibians–are cold-blooded and use gills to breathe in the water when they are young and lungs to breathe on land when they are adults

Reptiles–are covered in scales or bony plates and usually lay soft-shelled eggs on land

Mammals–have hair, make milk to feed their babies, and are warm-blooded

➡ **There are examples of each of the major groups of vertebrates below. Draw a line from each group (found in the boxes) to the correct animal.**

| Fish | Birds | Amphibians | Reptiles | Mammals |

ANCIENT GREECE

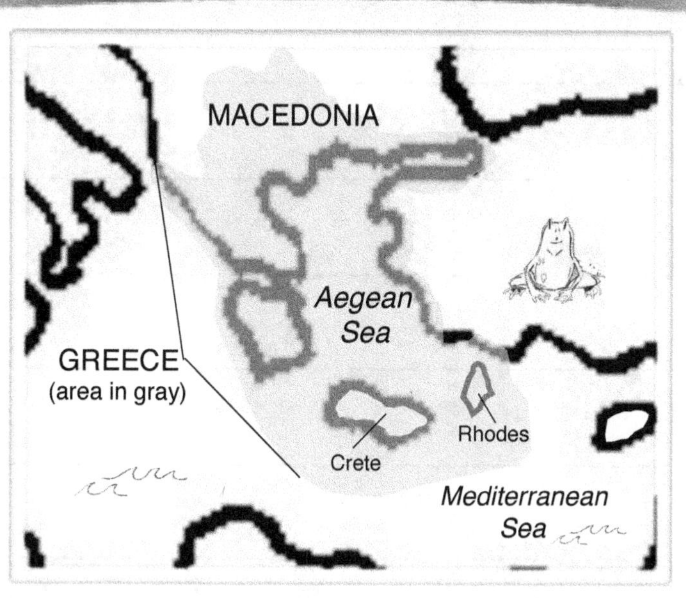

MAP IT!

Mediterranean tree frogs, like Fernando, live near the Mediterranean Sea. Color the areas of Ancient Greece where they could be found.

1. Color Greece YELLOW.

2. Color the Aegean Sea BLUE.

3. Color Macedonia RED.

4. Color Crete GREEN.

5. Color Rhodes PURPLE.

F6

GRACE THE GOOSE

BEAUTY IN INDIA

The lotus flower is very special to the people who live in India, and it is named their national flower. It grows in water, such as a pond, and has waxy leaves that help it to float. The petals are usually white or pink. The entire flower, including the stem and seeds, can be used as food and medicine. Even though it grows in murky water, it remains pristine and beautiful, which symbolizes that people can be too, even in the hardships they may face.

The lotus flower has been cherished in India for thousands of years and is used in their art and writings. Here is a lotus flower for you to decorate.

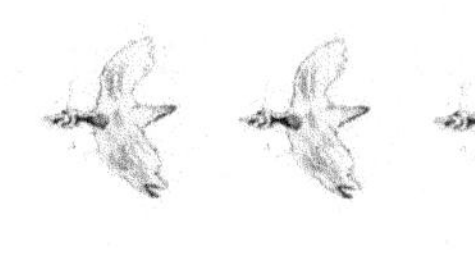

GEESE

1. egg   2. gosling   3. adult goose

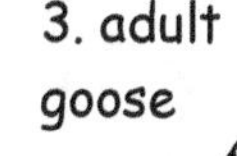

webbed feet for swimming

If you hear a honking noise outside your house, it's probably a goose. Geese are large birds that like to live in open places close to water. Bar-headed geese, like Grace, are big and gray, with two black stripes on their white heads. They also have yellow-orange beaks and feet.

Bar-headed geese usually fly high over Asia, their home; very high! They can even fly over Mt. Everest, the tallest mountain in the world! They just need to be careful not to bump their heads on airplanes! Unless they take a vacation to Rome like Grace did, they like to stay between China and India.

These geese mostly eat parts of plants: roots, seeds, leaves, and grasses; but they also like to eat some bugs and other insects. Mommy geese, like Grace's sister, usually lay clutches of four to six eggs. A few days after they hatch, these goslings, or baby geese, are already able to leave the nest and feed themselves!

Geese like to eat, but there are also creatures that like to eat goose! Animals like raccoons like goose eggs for breakfast, and bigger creatures like coyotes, foxes, and even crows attack full-grown geese! That's why bar-headed geese have two different danger calls: one for land predators and one for birds.

Draw a bar-headed goose flying over the tallest mountain in the world.

www.letslearnkids.com

© 2018 Hosanna Rodriguez

GEESE

What do I eat?

What is something special I can do?

What else do you know about me?

Draw and decorate your own goose egg.

www.letslearnkids.com

BABIES!

Reproduction means more are produced. There are different ways that reproduction happens in life.

Here are some of the ways animals reproduce:

Live birth–most mammals reproduce by live birth, including humans

Eggs–the mother lays an egg and the baby in an egg does most or all of its growing inside the egg; most fish, amphibians, reptiles, a few mammals, and all birds reproduce this way

Fragmentation–part of the parent detaches, producing a new creature; sea stars and some reproduce this way

Budding–cells split and gather on the parent, creating a new life, which eventually separates from the parent; freshwater organisms such as hydra reproduce this way

➡ **Here are some examples of each of the types of reproduction mentioned earlier. Draw a line from each group (found in the boxes) to the picture.**

| Live birth | Eggs | Fragmentation | Budding |

ROMAN EMPIRE

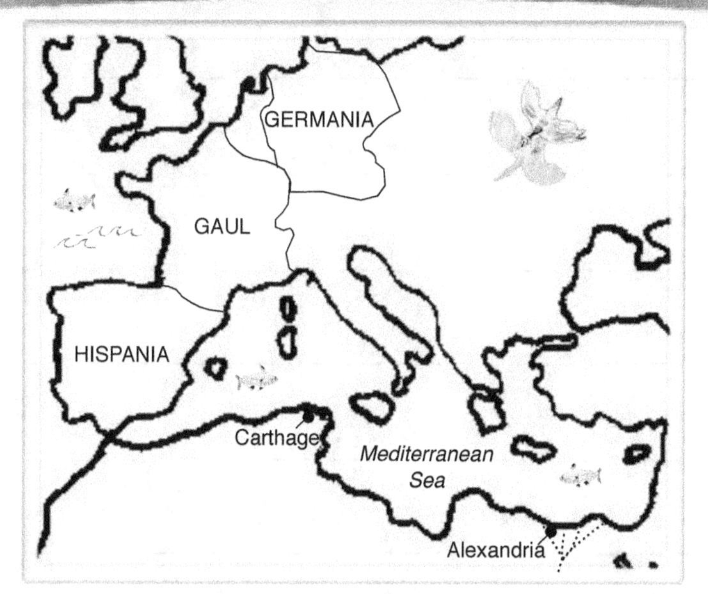

MAP IT!

Grace the Goose loved to vacation! Color some of the places she visited.

1. Color Germania RED.

2. Color Gaul ORANGE.

3. Color Hispania YELLOW.

4. Circle Carthage in GREEN.

5. Circle Alexandria in PURPLE.

HARRISON & HUTCH THE HORSES

H1

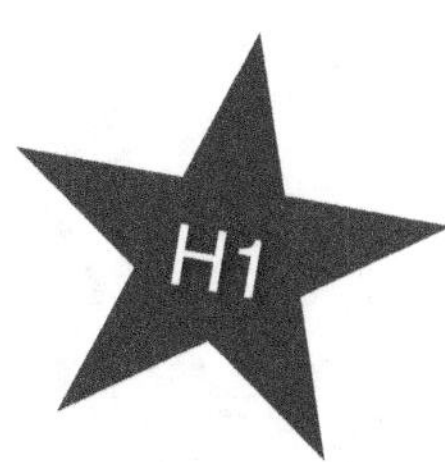

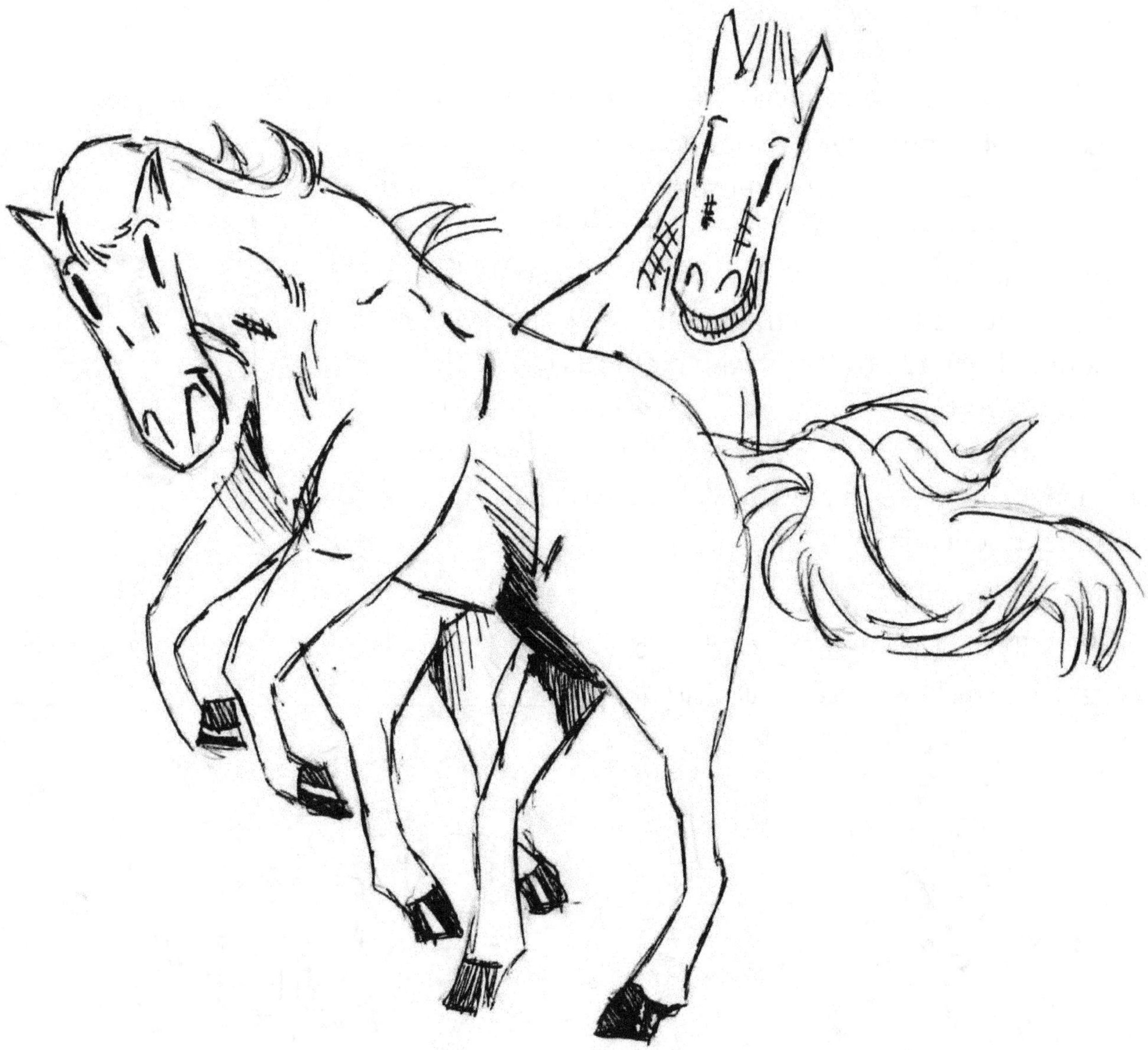

INDIA WINS ITS INDEPENDENCE

Exotic spices, cotton, tea, coffee and many more wonderful things come from India, which is why some have come, sometimes from faraway places, hoping to claim it as their own. There were the Muslim and Afghan Mughal rulers many years ago. Then the British began ruling in 1858. Queen Victoria, who was declared Empress of India in 1877, rode in the famous Gold State Coach that you see below, pulled by her trusty Windsor Grey horses.

There was an Indian man by the name of Mahatma Gandhi who fought to gain Independence from Britain, as well as to bring peace between Hindus and Muslims, and also to stop the bad treatment of the poor. He wanted India to be a place where people could live in peace and be treated fairly. Instead of fighting with guns, though, he made his point with methods like hunger strikes, which were times when he refused to eat in order to get the attention needed to make a change. He did make a change, and eventually India won its independence in 1947.

It's time to give the horses a treat!
All this talk about no eating is making Harrison and Hutch hungry! There is an empty crate below for horse treats. If you could, what treats would you give them? ____

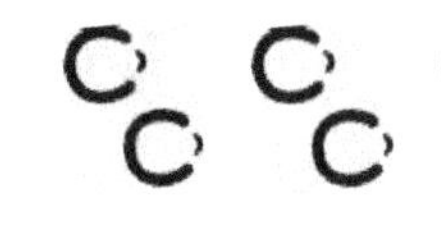

HORSES

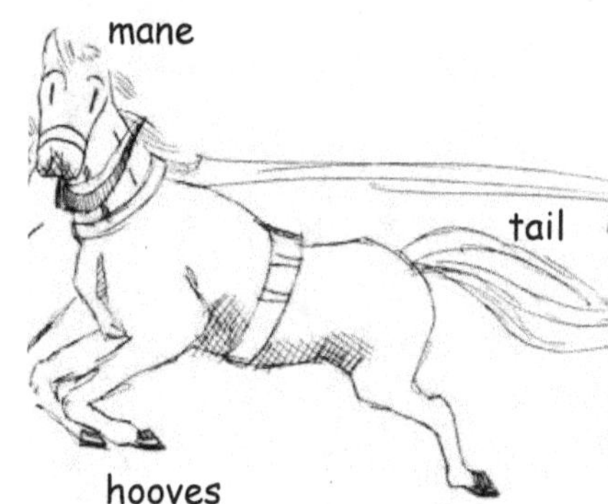

Horses are large, powerful animals, and they are very, very fast. They have beautiful skin and one hard toe on each foot, called a hoof. They are also related to the rhinoceros and a funny little creature called the tapir. With their long legs, they can run at different speeds for long periods of time.

Horses are also very smart, and they have been tamed by humans for a long time. In England, Windsor Grey horses, like Harrison and Hutch, are used for royal occasions. Only the most patient and calm horses are picked for the job, but they have to be trained first. Sometimes they might look a little silly with all the golden straps and eye-flaps on their gray bodies, but don't tell Harrison and Hutch that!

Most horses only sleep about three hours a day, and they do it standing up! This might seem uncomfortable, but it's easier to get away from other animals that want to eat them that way. When they are scared, they can run up to fifty miles per hour for a short time! That's almost as fast as a car on a freeway!

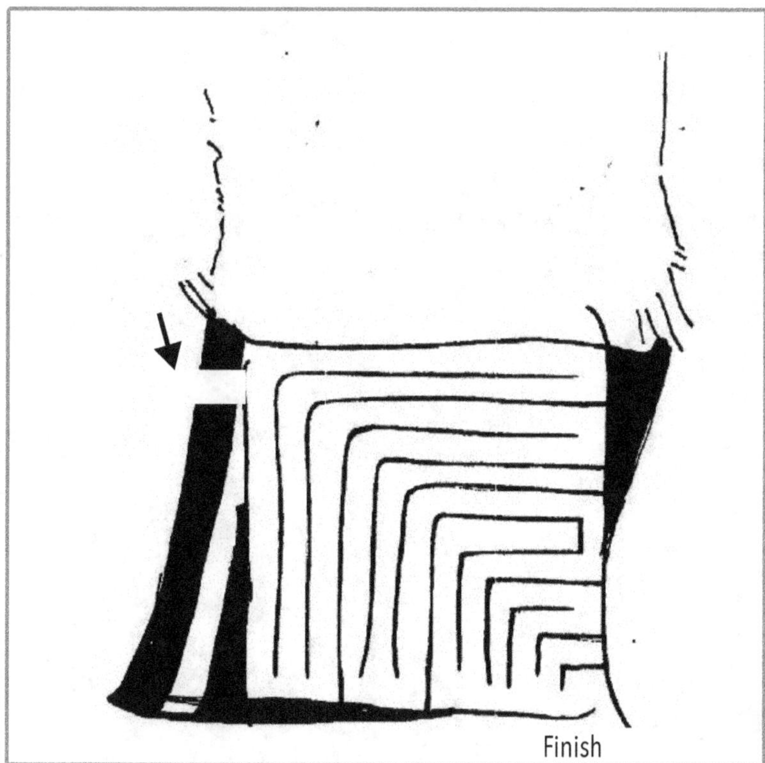

Here is a real challenge for you. Draw a picture of a bed for a creature who sleeps standing up.

HORSES

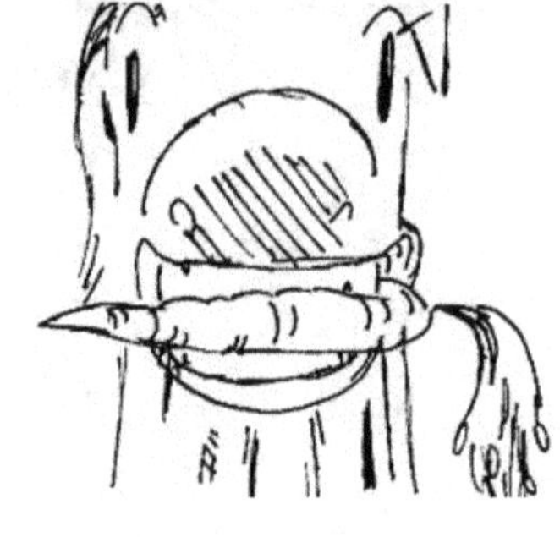

What do I eat?

How do I sleep?

What else do you know about me?

How fast can I run?

© 2018 Hosanna Rodriguez

WHO'S HUNGRY FOR SEED PLANTS?

Most plants on this planet are seed plants, meaning they grow from seeds.

Here are some types of seed plants:

Monocots–have flower parts in multiples of three (maybe three, or six, or even nine); some examples include onions, rice, corn, and so on

Dicots–have flower parts in multiples of five (maybe four); some examples include peaches, apples, cabbage, and so on

Conifers–are trees that spread their seeds from cones, and they are evergreen trees, often with needlelike leaves

There are some seed plants that horses would like to eat more than others. I have a feeling they wouldn't care for pinecones as much. Please match up the types of seed plants in the boxes by drawing a line to the pictures below. This way we'll know which ones to avoid feeding the horses—conifers!

| Monocots | Dicots | Conifers |

INDUS RIVER VALLEY

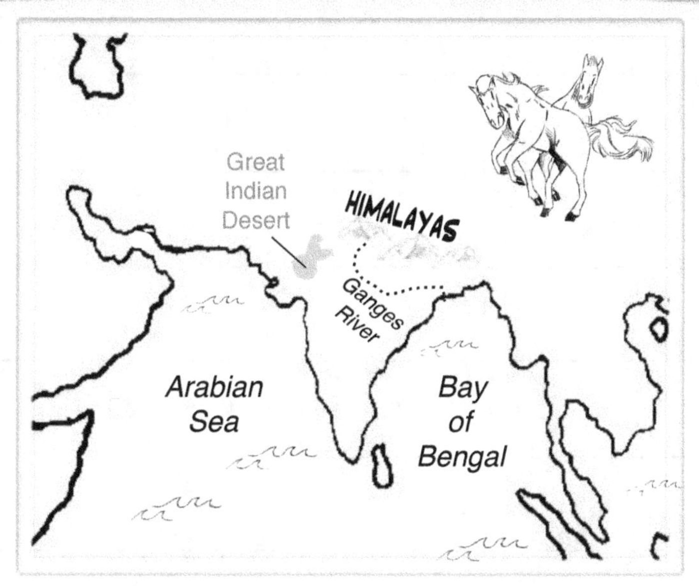

MAP IT!

Color all the places Harrison the Horse wanted to explore.

1. Color the Arabian Sea BLUE.

2. Color the Bay of Bengal GREEN.

3. Color the Ganges River PURPLE.

4. Color the Great Indian Desert RED.

5. Circle the Himalayas in ORANGE.

H6

IZZY THE IBIS

DRAGONS IN CHINA

China is a large country where many people live. Animals like the giant panda and crested ibis are important to them.

Another thing that they enjoy is a dragon dance performed at the end of every Chinese New Year parade. Dragons represent wisdom, power, and wealth to the Chinese. During the dance, performers hold the dragon up on poles, making him dance as they wind through the crowds of people to the sounds of horns, drums, and gongs. The Chinese dragon is very different than the Western dragon. It has the tail of a fish, the scales of a carp, the neck of a snake, the claws of an eagle, and the paws of a tiger. For the Chinese dragon costume, different colors can be chosen. The main body could be yellow to represent the empire, green for a good harvest, and red for excitement.

It's your turn!
Choose colors to design your own Chinese dragon.

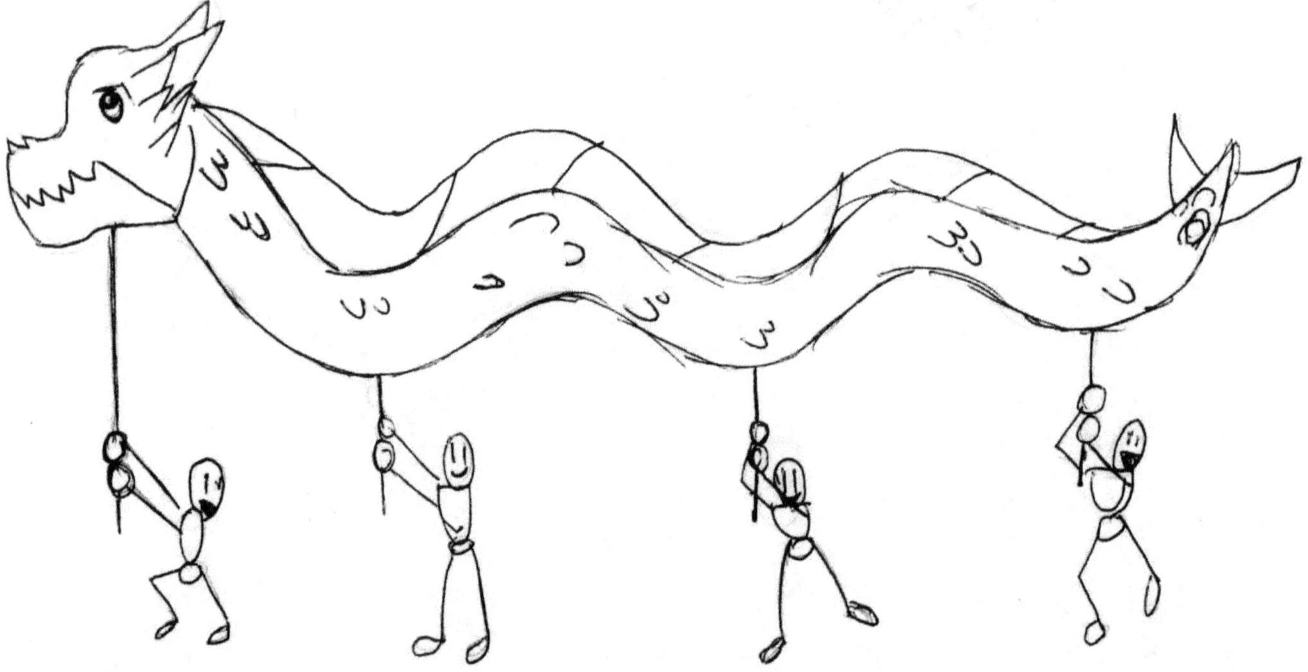

IBISES

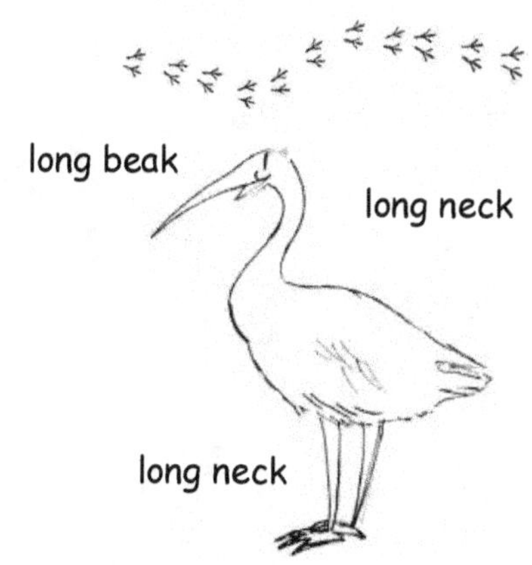

Ibises are funny birds that live and eat near water. There are 28 species of ibis, and all have different colors. They can be black, brown, grey, or white. Some ibises are red-orange or pink, and they get this color because of small creatures in the food they eat.

Ibises have long, thin legs and long, curved bills to scoop up their food from the mud. They can even breathe when their bills are underwater! Ibises have webbed feet to help them move around in the water, and they eat foods like fish, frogs, worms, and plants that live near water, so they like to stay near rivers and lakes. No wonder Izzy liked it in her wet, bamboo forest.

Many people like ibises in their fields and farms, because they eat lots of pesky bugs that might eat the farmer's plants. However, many kinds of ibis are endangered, meaning there aren't many of them left, so they have to work together to protect themselves. They are mostly quiet, and they live in groups to avoid being eaten by cats, foxes, snakes, and bigger birds. Izzy, however, is so loud, she could talk the beak right off an eagle!

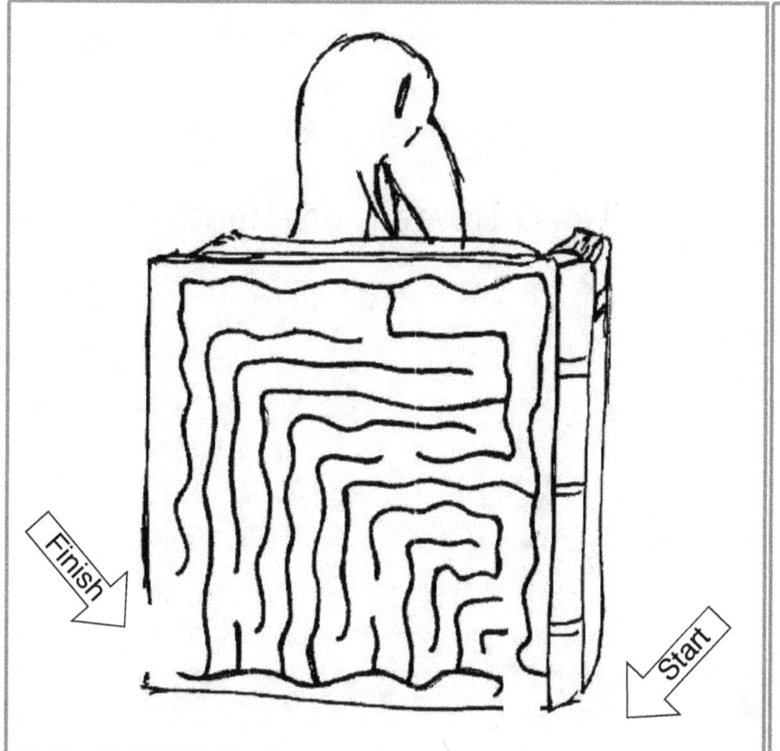

Draw an ibis in a bamboo forest.

IBISES

What do I eat?

Where do I live?

What else do you know about me?

Why do I have a long and curved bill?

WOULD ANYONE LIKE A CARROT?

When a plant has leaves, a stem, and roots, it is called a vascular plant. Those without all three of those parts, such as mosses, are called nonvascular plants.

Here are the functions of the three parts of vascular plants:

Leaves–the food factory of the plant, using sunlight and carbon dioxide

Stems–support the leaves and move the water and minerals from the roots upward, while moving the food downward to the roots

Roots–anchor the plant in the ground and soak up the water and nutrients

➤ **Do you know what kind of plant is in this picture? It's a carrot! First label the three parts of the plant, and then write below which part of the carrot plant we eat:**

We eat the: _________________________

CHINA

MAP IT!

Color the places Izzy the Ibis told her friends about.

1. Color Mongolia RED.

2. Color China PINK.

3. Color the Yellow River BLUE.

4. Color the Yangtze River GREEN.

5. Color the Yellow Sea YELLOW.

JADEN & JORDAN THE JAGUARS

J1

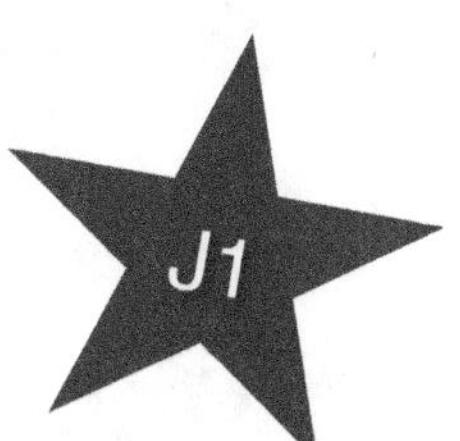

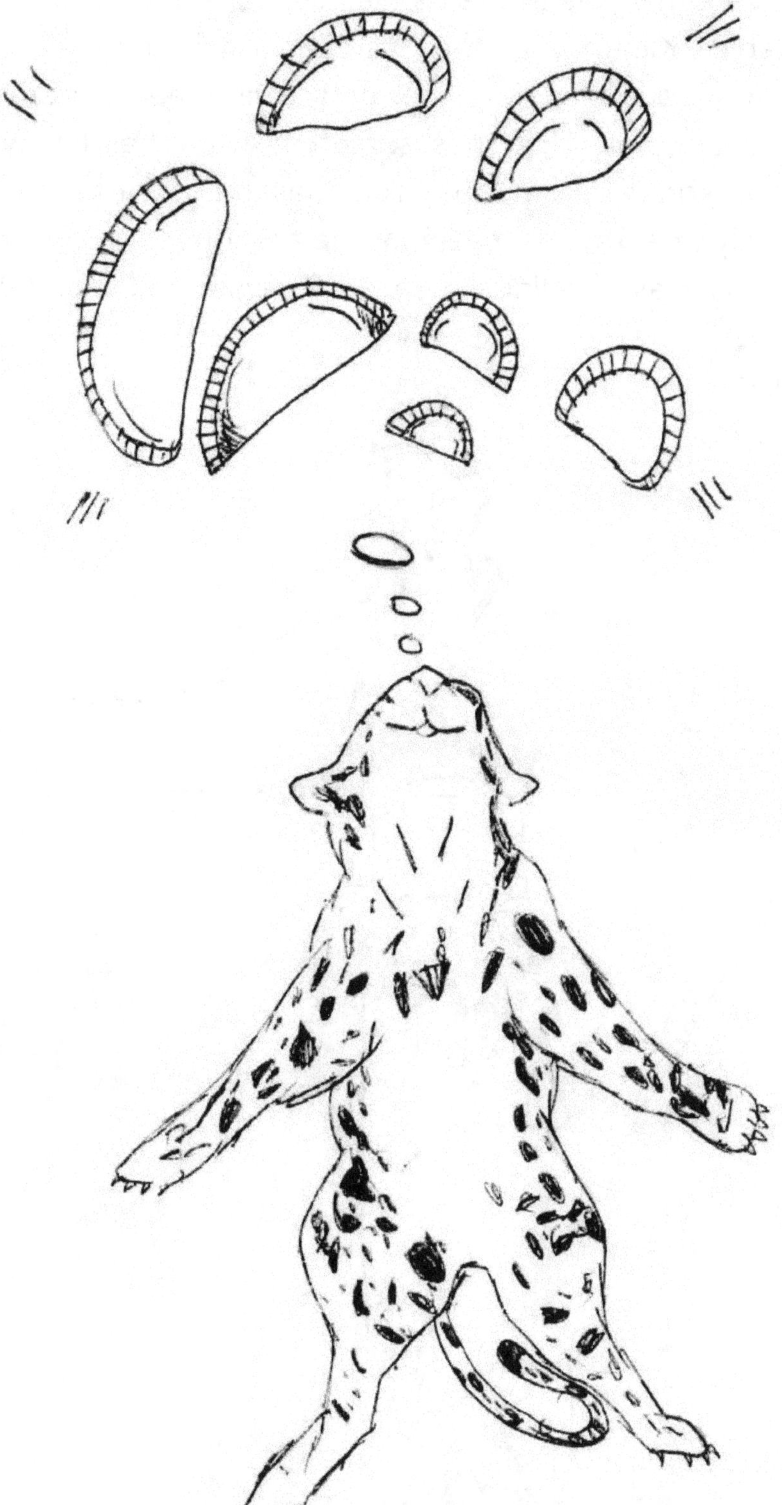

CLOTHING IN JAPAN

Japan is an archipelago, or a string of islands. Much of Japan is covered with mountains, and there are many earthquakes there. The people of Japan eat a lot of rice, fish, and vegetables. Kimonos are their traditional style of clothing. Making a kimono involves cutting fabric in straight lines and sewing them together. Both men and woman wear brightly colored kimonos, sometimes with their family crest, which showed their family background. Kimono-making has turned into an art form, and even though they rarely wear them in everyday life any longer, they still wear them for special occasions, such as weddings, funerals, festivals, and tea ceremonies.

Become a kimono designer!
Choose colors to design your own
Japanese kimono.

JAGUARS

rosette spots

large paws

The third-largest cat in the world, after the tiger and the lion, is the jaguar. Jaguars are large, heavy creatures, with beautiful, rose-shaped black spots called rosettes on their tan skin. They are skilled hunters, and their name means "he who catches with one leap."

Being hunters, jaguars eat lots of meat and fish, which they scoop up out of the water with their large paws. They are so fierce and powerful that no other creature would mess with a jaguar! However, other jaguars might steal their food, so they mark their territory by slashing trees, saying "you'd better not come in here!"

As fierce and beautiful as they are, jaguars have been hunted by humans for their colorful skin for hundreds of years. This is exactly what happened to Jaden and Jordan. Unfortunately, not many escape like our two jaguar friends did, and so jaguars are endangered, and they have to be protected so that they don't die out.

Draw your own pattern of jaguar rosette spots.

JAGUARS

J4

What do I eat?

What do I do?

What else do you know about me?

What is a danger to me?

SO MANY LEAVES! 

Last time we learned that leaves make the food for plants. Leaves also help us identify a plant based on the shape, color, and other details.

➡ **There are many different shapes of leaves. Some shapes are shown below. Draw each of the leaves in the empty boxes.**

Linear Leaf	**Oval Leaf**	**Lobed Leaf**
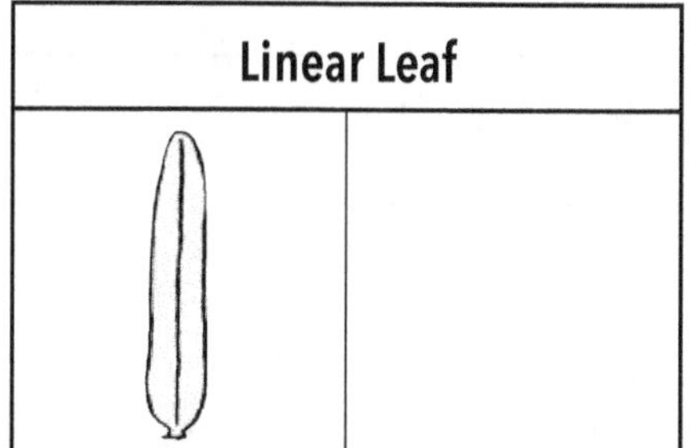	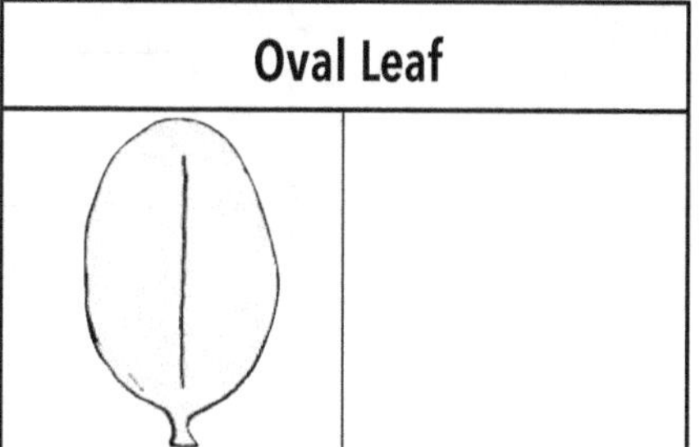	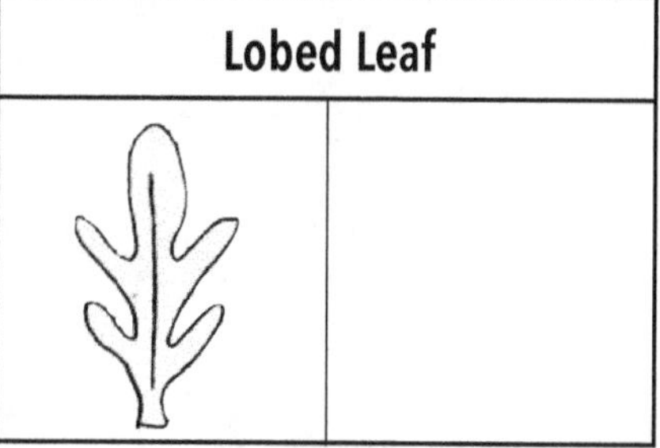

Cleft Leaf	**Scalelike Leaf**	**Needlelike Leaf**
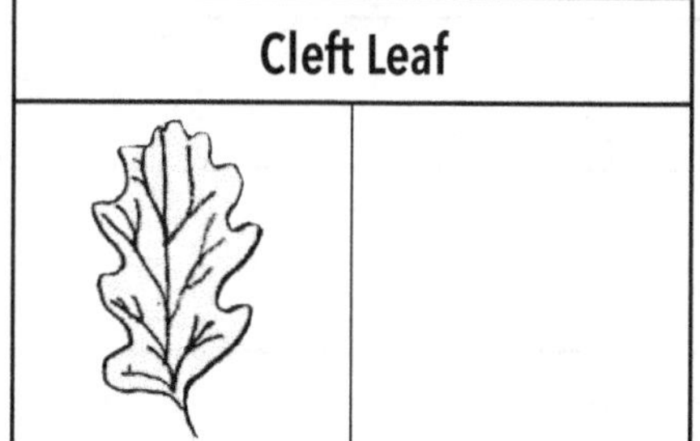	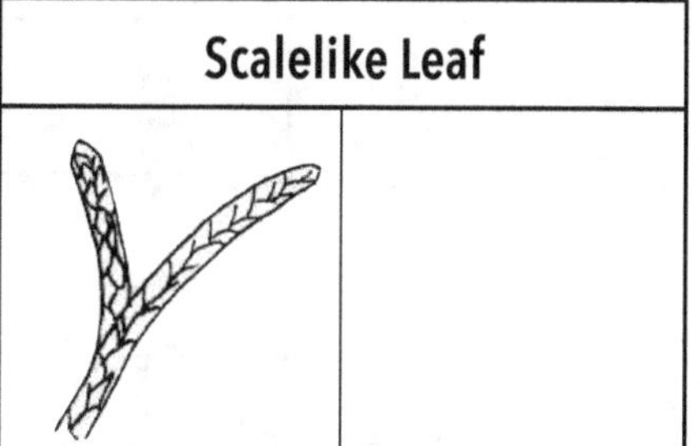	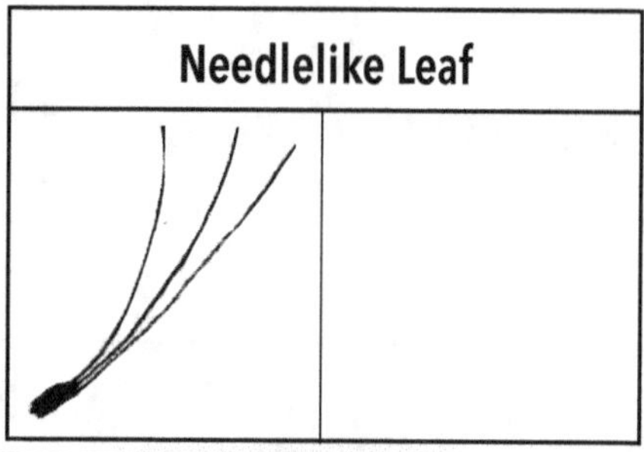

JAPAN

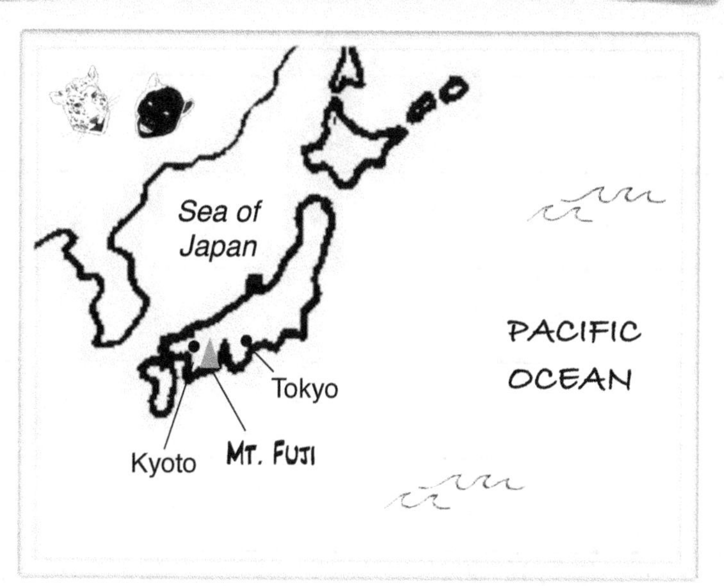

MAP IT!

Jordan and Jaden the Jaguars were captured and taken to Kyoto, Japan. Color the places they left behind to get back home.

1. Color the Sea of Japan GREEN.

2. Color the Pacific Ocean BLUE.

3. Circle Tokyo in PURPLE.

4. Circle Mt. Fuji in RED.

5. Circle Kyoto in ORANGE.

J6

KEILY THE KANGAROO

HIDE-AND-GO-SEEK AT THE HAGIA SOPHIA

The Hagia Sophia is the most important Byzantine structure and one of the world's great monuments. It was first built by Emperor Constantine in AD 360. It had a wooden roof, and it eventually burned down. The building was rebuilt in AD 415 when the Byzantine emperor Justinian I ruled. It was originally built as a Christian church, but after the Ottoman Turks conquered the empire in 1453, it was turned into a mosque. It is now a museum. Its original location was called Constantinople, but it is now known as Istanbul, Turkey. This gigantic architectural wonder has a dome that stretches high into the air, a marble floor, and mosaics made from gold, silver, glass, and colorful stones showing scenes and figures from the Christian Gospels. Many of these mosaics were covered when it was turned into a mosque after Constantinople was captured by the Ottomans since Islam was their religion.

Help Keily the Kangaroo find her friends–Barend the Bear, Jaden and Jordan the Jaguars, and Amber the Ant.

KANGAROOS

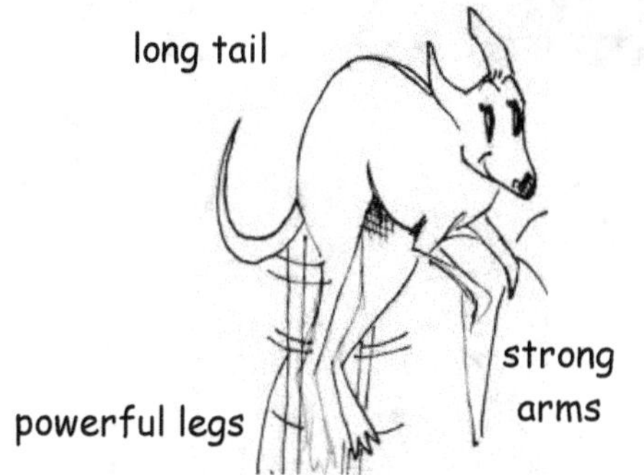

Our friend Keily is an eastern gray kangaroo. There are three other kinds: red kangaroos, western gray kangaroos, and antilopine kangaroos. These animals have long ears and powerful legs, and they are the largest animals with a pouch in the world.

There are many things kangaroos can do; they can leap forward forty feet, they can jump up three times their hight, they can hop on two legs or walk on all four, and they can even swim! But there is one thing they cannot do: they cannot walk backward. That's one thing you can do that a kangaroo can't. Of course, if you told a kangaroo that, they would probably kick you in the stomach!

Kangaroos mainly eat grass, which gives them their amazing energy. When kangaroos form a group with their joeys, or baby kangaroos, it's called a mob! Sometimes they're called a troop or a court. Watch out for the kangaroo court when they come around!

Of the many things kangaroos can do, draw what you would like to see them do.

KANGAROOS

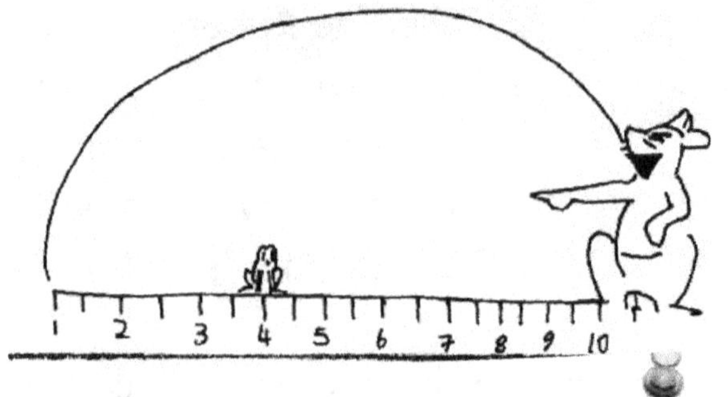

What do I eat?

What do I do?

What else do you know about me?

What is my baby called?

STOP TO SMELL THE FLOWERS

There are many different kinds of flowers. They come in different shapes, sizes, and colors, and some even smell beautiful! There are some things that flowers have similarities in, however, and that's their parts.

Here are some parts of a flower:

Petal–attracts insects, so that pollen can be moved from one flower to the next

Sepal–the outer covering of the flower's base

Pistil–contains the seeds

Stamen–usually is made up of the anther and a stalk

Anther–produces pollen

➡ **Most flowers are colorful. Let's color your flower below. Color the sepal green, the pistil yellow, the anther brown, the stalk of the stamen green, and the petal whatever color you would like.**

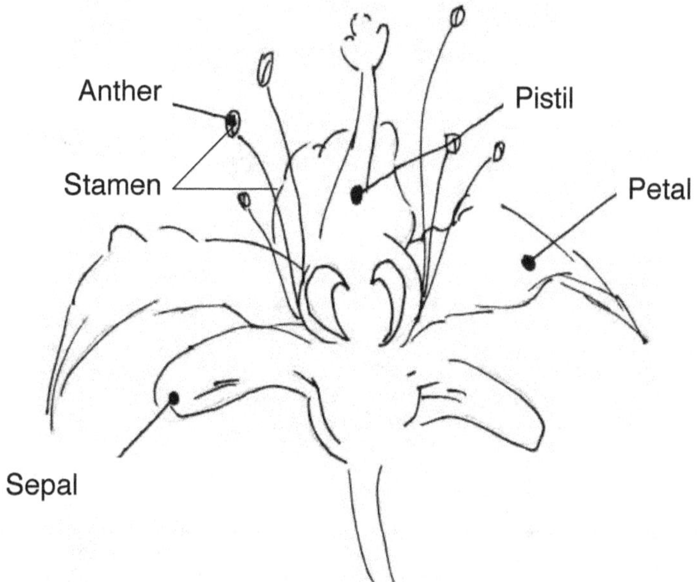

BYZANTINE EMPIRE

MAP IT!

When Keily the Kangaroo traveled with her new friends, it was her first faraway trip. Color the places her friends had already been.

1. Circle Rome in RED.

2. Circle Athens in ORANGE.

3. Circle Constantinople in GREEN.

4. Circle Ephesus in BLUE.

5. Circle Antioch in PURPLE.

K6

LENNY THE LADYBUG

LENNY VISITS A MOSQUE

One of the sights Lenny the Ladybug wanted to see on his vacation was a Muslim mosque. When he finally made it to one of these houses of prayer, he saw the Persian prayer rugs and the flags with a star and a crescent moon. The star and the crescent were a symbol of the Ottoman Turks. As the Ottoman Turks expanded the Muslim Empire by conquering places like Constantinople, the star and the crescent began to represent the Muslim religion—Islam.

Lenny the Ladybug dreamt he was so strong that he could lift the mosque with one hand! After coloring the picture, see what you can lift with one hand.

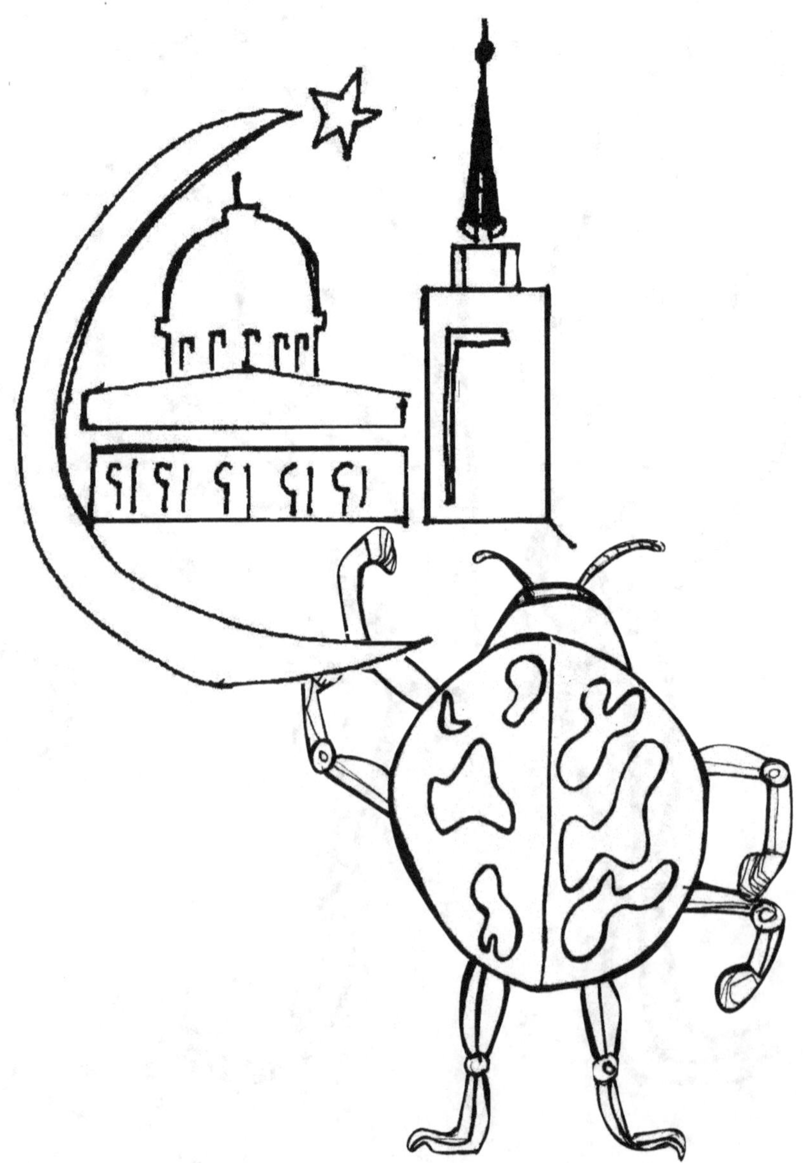

LADYBUGS

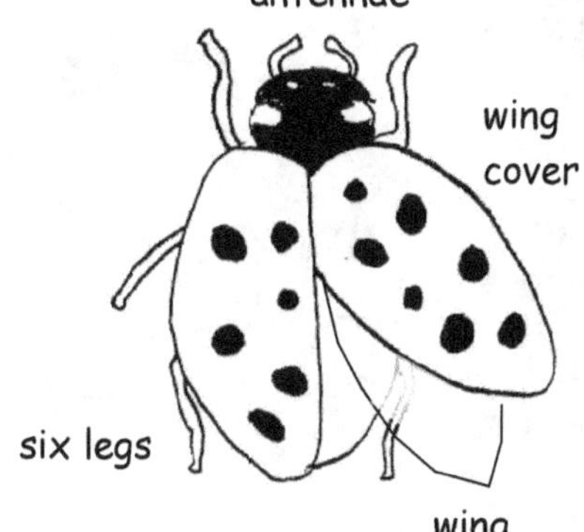

Ladybugs aren't only ladies; some are female and some are male. These beetles have shells that can be red-orange or other colors, with anywhere from zero to twenty black spots! It gets difficult to count them, though, when their outer shell splits open and the inner set of wings unfold to fly.

A ladybug starts out as a tiny yellow egg on a leaf. The egg gradually grows white, and then what looks like a little black alligator with six legs crawls out of it. They grow bigger and bigger, shedding their skin, until they fasten themselves down into a pupa, a sort of cocoon, and emerge as a ladybug!

Now about Lenny's famous sprayers. Ladybugs spray a stinky yellow liquid out of their front legs to warn off predators. Their orange color warns that they might taste bad or even be poisonous. They may also play dead. In the winter, they hibernate in order to not freeze. They have lots of ways to keep safe!

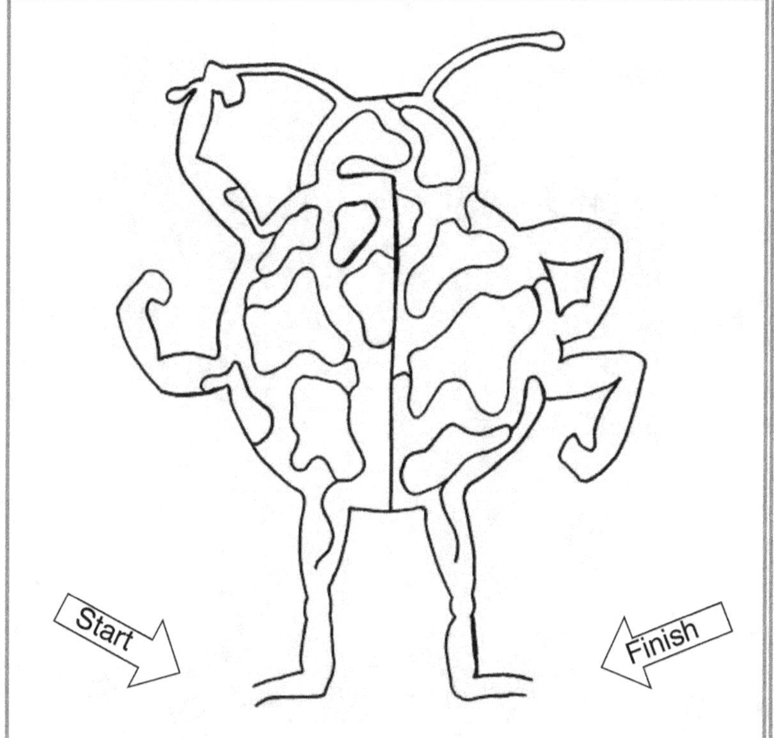

Draw a bed for Lenny to sleep in when it's time for him to hibernate.

LADYBUGS

L4

How many spots can I have?

Are all ladybugs ladies?

What else do you know about me?

How do I protect myself?

WE ALL NEED PLANTS

Did you know that we all need plants, and that they need us too? We need the oxygen that they give off, and they need the carbon dioxide that we breathe out in order to make food. It's one of several steps, or systems, that plants use to function.

Here are some systems of plants:

Photosynthesis–when plants make their own food using water, sunlight, and carbon dioxide

Respiration–when plants take in oxygen through the leaves and roots to create energy, which happens throughout the day, but mostly when there is no sunlight

Transpiration–when water is absorbed by the roots, travels through the plant, and exits through the leaves, allowing carbon dioxide to get into the leaves

The sun is out, and photosynthesis for this plant is in full action. Lenny is looking for a blast of oxygen coming from the plant. Draw the oxygen coming out of the plant so Lenny can breathe it in.

MUSLIM EMPIRE

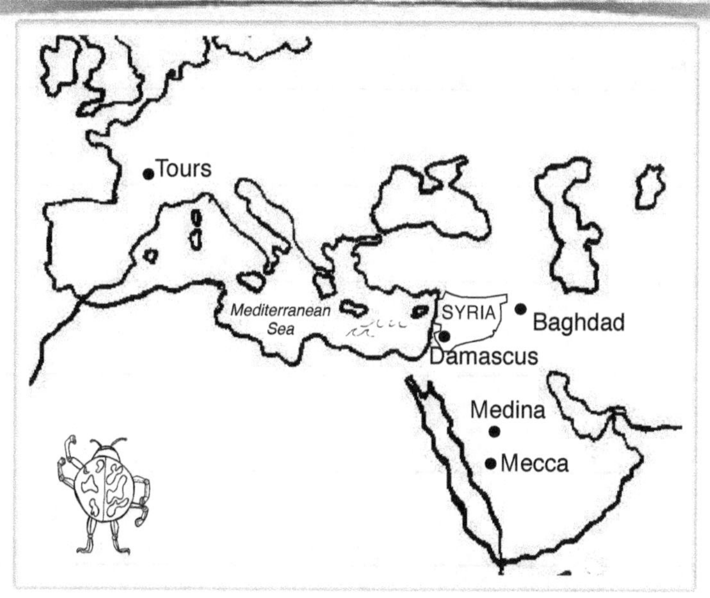

MAP IT!

Ella the Eagle searched the first four locations below while Lenny the Ladybug was learning about the last two. Color them on the map.

1. Circle Tours in PURPLE.

2. Color Syria YELLOW.

3. Circle Damascus in RED.

4. Circle Baghdad in GREEN.

5. Circle Medina in ORANGE.

6. Circle Mecca in BROWN.

L6

MARLA THE MOUSE

IT'S A GOLD RUSH AT THE NILE!

Marla the Mouse joined the Kush people in mining gold along the Nile River in Egypt. There was so much of the shiny treasure that they needed containers to collect it all in.

They are scooping up the gold pieces below in 1-quart containers and pouring the gold into the 1-gallon buckets. If 4 quarts equal 1 gallon, how many of the 1-quart containers of gold will they need to fill both of the 1-gallon buckets?

____

Note: You may see gold coins scattered around the buckets below, but the gold they found along the river would really have been collected as nuggets. Making coins out of gold would have involved pounding and other steps to make it into coins.

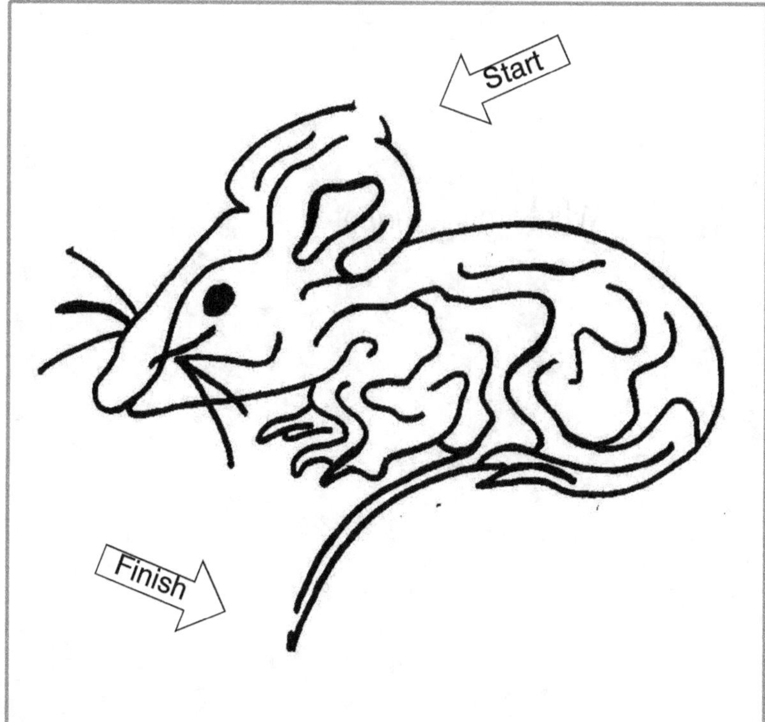

Marla is now the world's most popular Cairo spiny mouse, one of the sixty kinds of mice on the planet. All mice have pointed noses, small, round ears, and long, bald tails. These can be as long as the mouse's body! Cairo spiny mice have short bristles all over their backs.

Though they can be skittish and timid, Cairo spiny mice keep their homes in the gravel plains tidy and neat, storing their food in a certain place and sleeping in a reserved area. These mice eat seeds, snails, and bugs. They use their whiskers to find out where they are and how hot or cold it is.

Mice, like Marla, are naturally timid because there are so many animals that want to eat them! Wild cats and dogs, snakes, birds, and lots of other animals find them a tasty treat. Marla can't be blamed for panicking when Ella, a fierce eagle and a bird of prey, picked her up into the sky.

Draw a Cairo spiny mouse with bristles on its back.

MICE

M4

What do I eat?

What kind of housekeeper am I?

What else do you know about me?

What am I scared of?

WHAT IN THE WORLD?

Our world can be split into layers, from the air above to the bodies of water and solid surfaces. The layers of the earth are:

Atmosphere–air around the earth

Biosphere–the part of the earth where living things are found, including the air, ground, and water

Hydrosphere–water on the surface of the earth, in the ground, and in the air

Crust–outer layer of the earth, where we live

Mantle–layer of the earth between the crust and the core

Core–some parts are liquid, and it's very hot, with the innermost part as hot as the surface of the sun

➡ **If you could take a slice of the earth like a slice of cheese, you would see all the layers, from the atmosphere, all the way down to the core.**

Where would Marla the Mouse live? _______________________

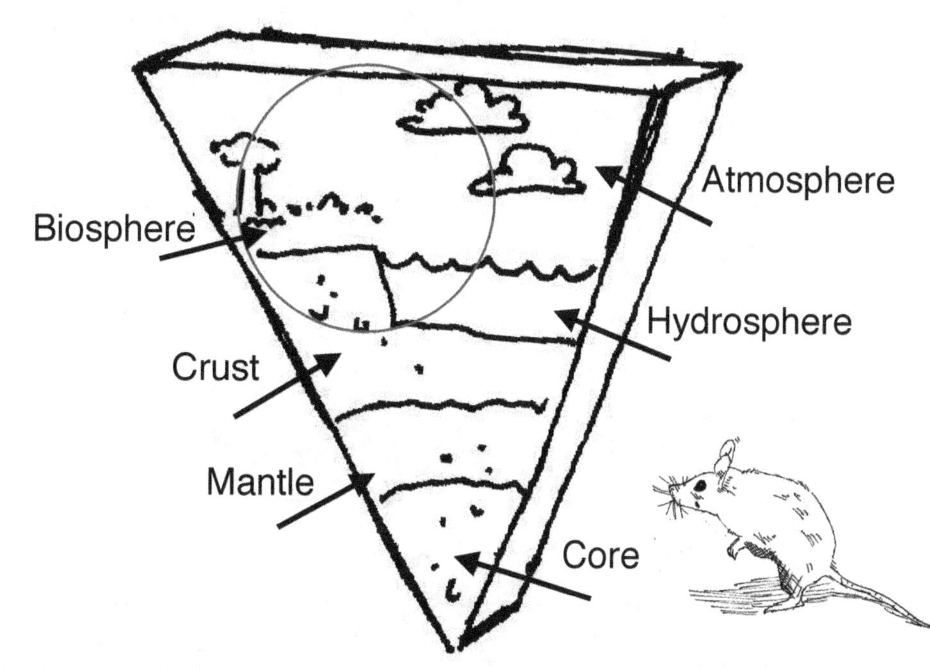

WESTERN AFRICA

MAP IT!

Lenny the Ladybug told Marla the Mouse that with the Stone, they could visit all of the places below. Color them on the map.

1. **Color the Sahara desert BROWN.**

2. **Color the Atlantic Ocean BLUE.**

3. **Color the Niger River PURPLE.**

4. **Color the Senegal River GREEN.**

5. **Color the Ivory Coast ORANGE.**

M6

NARI THE NEWT

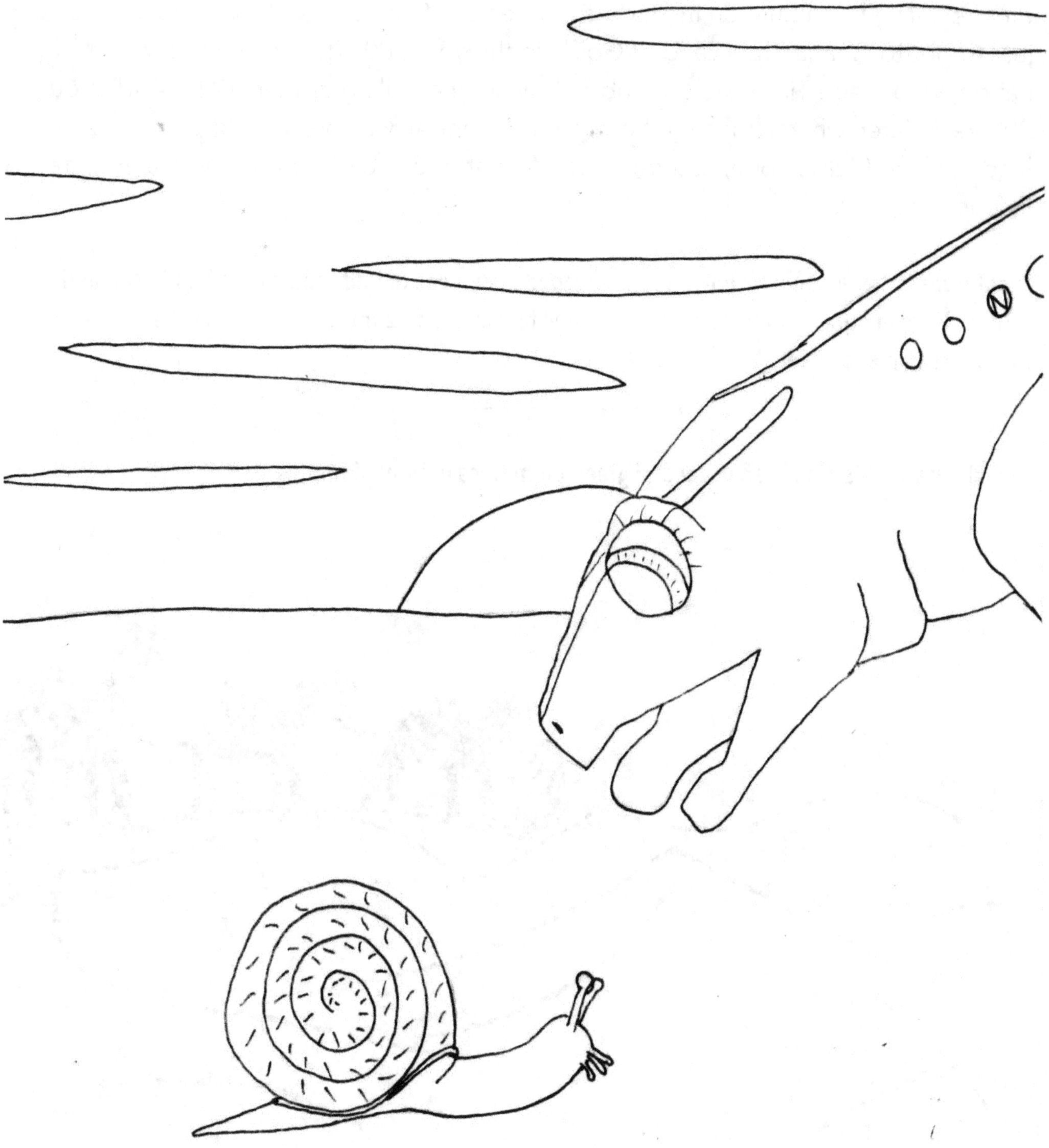

NOW CROSSING THE SAHARA FOR GOLD!

Gold must have been important throughout history, as it is now, because some empires have been built on it. Traders crossed the Sahara desert by camel caravans just to get to Ghana, the "Land of Gold" in the year 700. Then came the Mali nation, who made Timbuktu the hub of buying and selling gold in 1240. And about 200 years later, when a man by the name of Sunni Ali was being held prisoner by the leader of the Mali Empire, escaped and soon after established the Songhai Empire in western Africa.

Look! Here comes a Sunni Ali now! He has escaped and needs to find some water for himself and his camels. He is imagining there is water only three feet away. If 12 inches are in 1 foot, then how many inches are in 3 feet?

____

Now draw an oasis with fresh water and green palm trees in front of him.

NEWTS

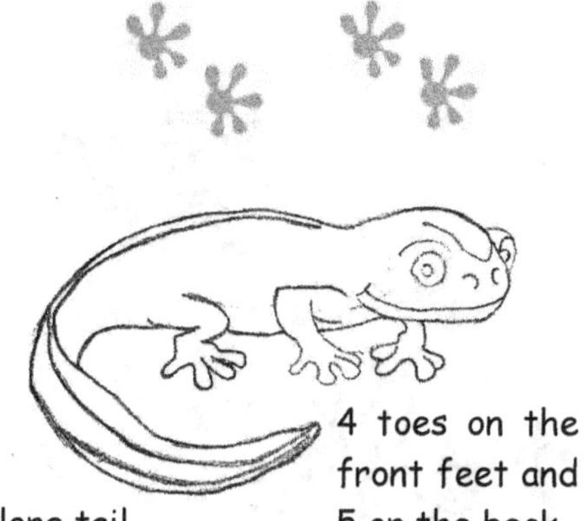

long tail

4 toes on the front feet and 5 on the back

Newts look like slimy lizards, with long tails and colorful bodies. Himalayan newts, like Nari, have moist, rough bodies, colored dark gray with red-orange spots, and their tails are usually a lighter color.

Most newts live in wet places, like Nari's home in India, and they can breathe underwater! They need to be near water to keep their skin nice and moist. There are four main types of newts: common newts, palmate newts, crested newts, and fire-bellied newts, like the ones Nari fought. Newts use their eyes to hunt, so they need to be able to see their food moving. Newts can't catch on fire like Nari, but they do have a poisonous layer of skin in case something tries to eat them.

Himalayan newts eat insects, worms, and snails, like the one Nari ate at the beginning of the story. Once mommy newts have eaten a lot and grown big, they can start laying eggs in pools or other bodies of water. Sometimes the mom wraps the eggs in leaves to protect them. Once they hatch, the mom takes care of them for a little while. Baby newts grow their front legs first, while frogs grow their hind legs first.

Draw a fire-bellied newt.

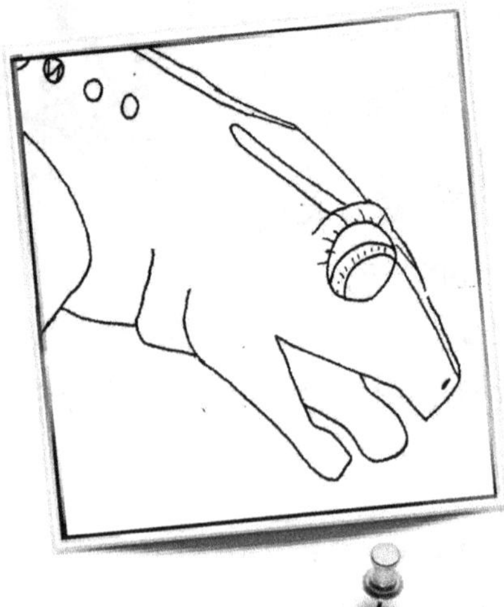

NEWTS

What do I eat?

What kind of environment do I like to live in?

What else do you know about me?

What do I have that helps me protect myself from danger?

WATCH OUT FOR FALLING ROCKS!

There are three main types of rock, and the differences among them have to do with how they formed.

Sedimentary–form from particles of sand, pebbles, and shells, and is usually the only type with fossils

Metamorphic–form under the surface of the earth, under intense heat and pressure

Igneous–form when magma (melted rock deep within the earth) cools and hardens

Out of all three types of rock, which one would you expect to crumble apart easily?

____

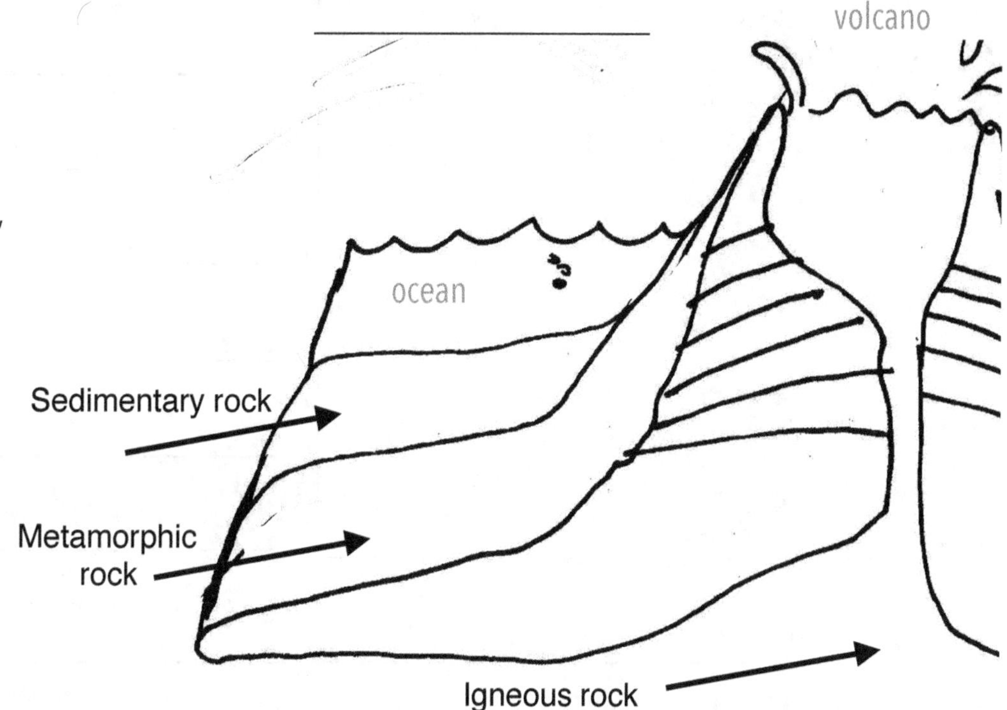

ANCIENT AFRICA

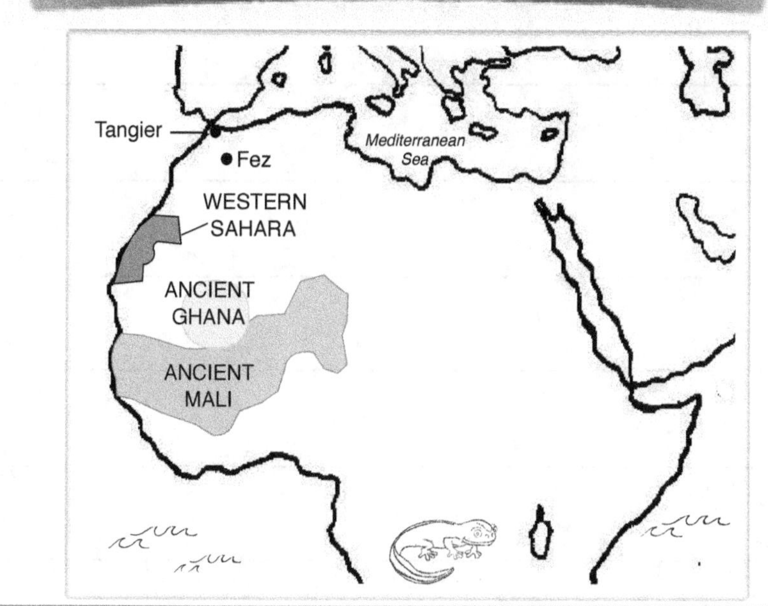

MAP IT!

Nari the Newt traveled across western Africa. Color the places she visited below.

1. Color Ancient Mali RED.

2. Color Ancient Ghana GREEN.

3. Color Western Sahara PURPLE.

4. Circle Fez in YELLOW.

5. Circle Tangier in ORANGE.

N6

OWEN THE OWL

SERPENTS IN THE SEA OF DARKNESS!

If you were a sailor from Europe who lived before the the 1400s, you most likely wouldn't have traveled past Cape Bojador on the western coast of Africa, because everyone knew there were serpents and monsters in the Sea of Darkness. Or, at least that's what they thought, because people who sailed south of Cape Bojador never seemed to return. The real reason was because of the violent storms and strong currents. Well, thankfully, things started to change when people like Prince Henry, or Henrique as they would say in his country of Portugal, began sending sailors down in caravels, ships that were speedy and maneuverable.

Can you find Owen the Owl on the caravel in this picture? After you find him, color the sea serpent, the ship, and the ocean water.

Owls are the silent hunters of the night. With their large bodies, scary orange-red eyes, and big ear tufts, Eurasian eagle owls, like Owen, are predators of almost anything that moves!

While Owen might be harmless, the owls of his kind sure aren't! These eagle owls have powerful talons, or claws, coated with feathers. Owls have special channels in their wings that help air slide through, making them silent as they fly.

Owls can eat basically anything smaller than they are, and they have great vision to see their food. But they can only see things far away—things up close seem fuzzy to them. Most owls have patterns on their skin that help them blend into their natural homes. Eurasian eagle owls have brown, gray, and black colors, markings, blotches, splotches, spots, bars, waves, stripes, and freckles similar to the colors of their homes in rocks, bushes, and dead trees. Even as young owlets, guarded in their nests by their parents, eagle owls have no natural predators, and they can live a very long time.

OWLS

04

What do I eat?

When am I awake?

What else do you know about me?

What do I have that helps me catch food?

MAKING MOUNTAINS OUT OF MOLE HILLS

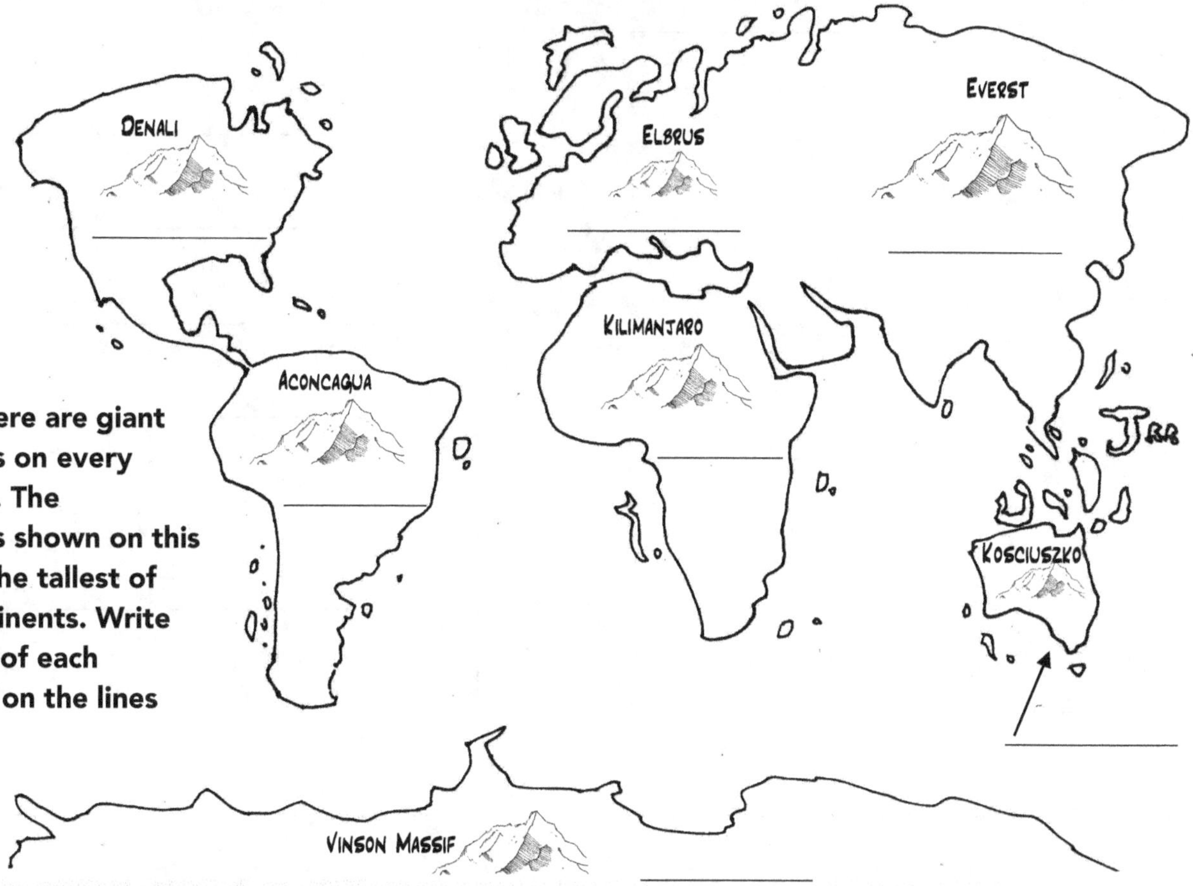

There are giant mountains on every continent. The mountains shown on this map are the tallest of their continents. Write the name of each continent on the lines provided.

MIDDLE EAST

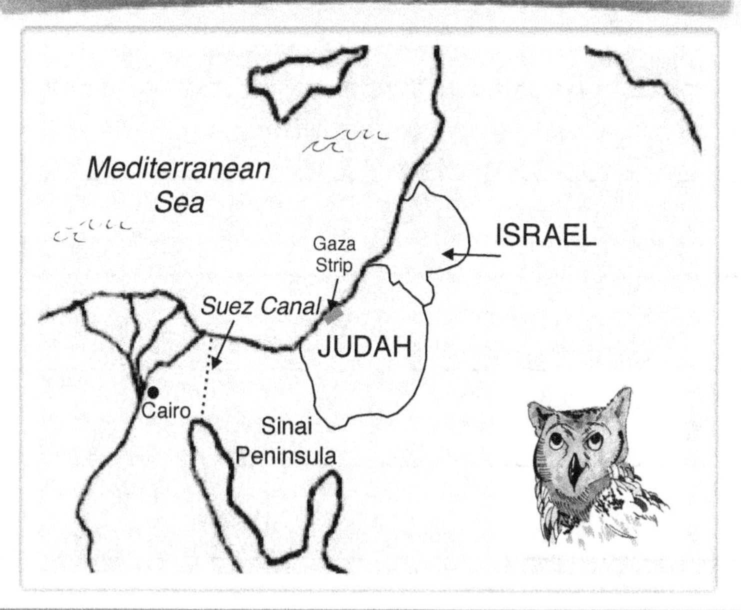

MAP IT!

As Owen the Owl and his new friends thought about Egypt, they also thought about the places nearby. Color those places listed below.

1. Color Israel PINK.

2. Color the Gaza Strip RED.

3. Color the Sinai Peninsula GREEN.

4. Color the Suez Canal BLUE.

5. Circle Cairo in ORANGE.

PARIC AND PAUL THE PIGEONS

ANCIENT TREASURES LEFT BEHIND

The Olmecs, Mayans, and Aztecs are all ancient civilizations of the western hemisphere. Even though they lived many years ago, the things they left behind are still intrigue us today. The Olmecs crafted giant relic statues in the shapes of heads. They were called colossal heads, were made of stone, and were nearly ten feet tall. The Mayans developed a paint they named after themselves called Maya Blue, which was made from clay and a plant called indigo. The Aztecs used weapons called macuahuitl, which were made of wood and volcanic stone embedded along the edges.

The club on the left was one used in the story of Paric and Paul the Pigeons. Design your own Aztec macuahuitl club on the right.

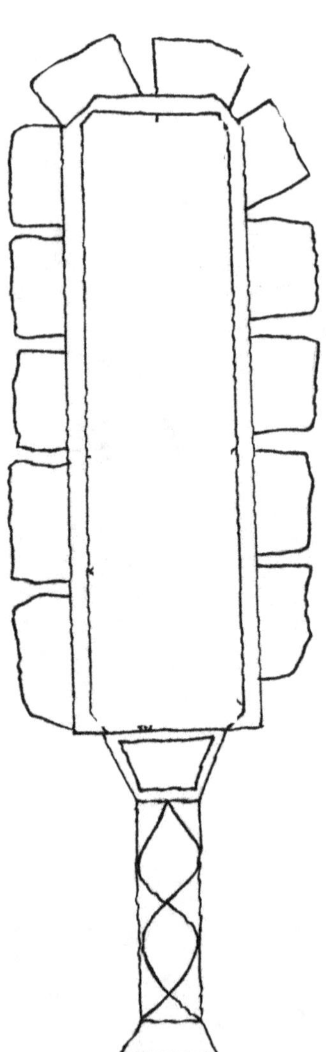

PIGEONS

Pigeons are very intelligent, for birdbrains! They have very sharp senses and beautiful features. Some people keep them as pets, but others, like Paric and Paul, like to have their own lives.

Red-billed pigeons, like Paric and Paul, have soft, grayish-blue feathers, with beautiful smudges of red. They are always looking for food on the ground or in bushes, and go up in the trees to find berries. They mainly eat seeds, nuts, certain plants, and other fruits.

Pigeons have some very special talents. With their strong muscles, pigeons can flap their wings ten times in a second! They can fly up to sixty miles per hour, and they can climb up to six thousand feet in the air! These amazing birds can hear storms and other natural activities from far away. They can see things almost thirty miles away! They also live in flocks, and they can identify different objects, even different letters in the alphabet!

Red-billed pigeons lay only one white egg at a time, but they can lay up to eight times each year in warm places. Couples, like Paric and Paul, work together building the nest and keeping the eggs warm. That's teamwork for you!

Draw Paric and Paul's nest with an egg they will have one day.

PIGEONS

What do I eat?

Where do I find my food?

What else do you know about me?

What are some great things I can do?

VOLCANOES ARE HOT STUFF

Volcanoes are mountains or hills that have a tunnel-like crater inside through which lava and vapors move, sometimes exploding out the top and pouring down the sides. People and animals may run from an erupting volcano, but a volcano isn't all bad. The ash left behind puts nutrients into the soil, which is good for plants. And plants are good for animals and people.

Here are some types of volcanoes:

Active–volcanoes that are currently erupting or that erupt regularly

Intermittent–volcanoes that erupt at regular time periods

Dormant–volcanoes that are not currently erupting, but are expected to erupt again

Extinct–volcanoes that haven't erupted in a long time and aren't expected to

Paric the Pigeon was worried a volcano was about to erupt near her and Paul's home. Can you figure out which type of volcano below is active, which is intermittent, which is dormant, and which is extinct? Write the answers on the lines below each volcano.

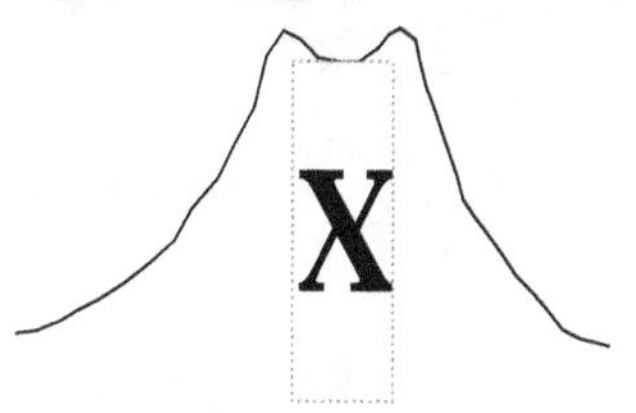

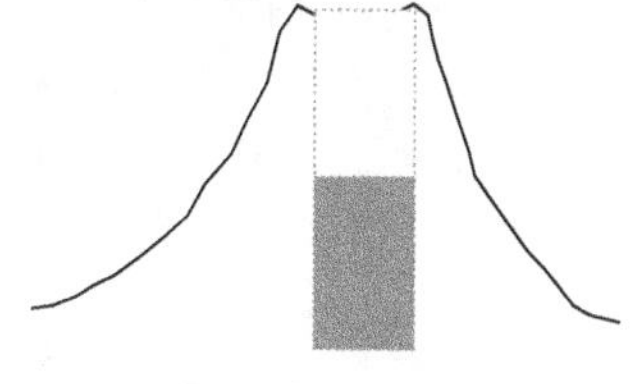

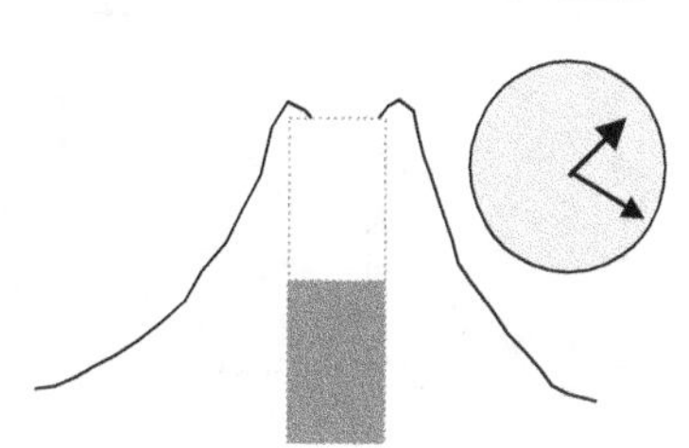

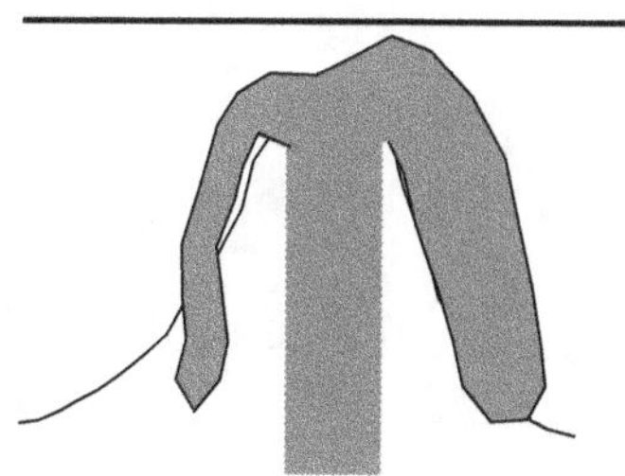

AFRICAN WATERS

MAP IT!

Amber told Paric and Paul the Pigeons about some of the places they had been with the Commandment Stone. Color them on the map.

1. Color Lake Victoria PURPLE.

2. Color the Congo River BLUE.

3. Color the Zambezi River GREEN.

4. Circle the Orange River in ORANGE.

QUINN THE QUAIL

COUNT THE STEPS OF THE AZTEC PYRAMID

When people think of pyramids, they often think of the pyramids in Egypt. An ocean voyage and a trek over land away, however, the Aztec civilization were building their own types of pyramids as others had done in that region for many years. There were three main types of pyramids that the Aztecs built. One, called the twin stairs pyramids, had a double set of stairs leading to the top and a square-shaped base. The second was a round pyramid, which was less common than the first. And finally there were the smaller types with only one set of stairs, but also with a square base, which were usually built in smaller cities. The pyramids were temples, and the Aztecs believed they were the homes of their gods. They continued to build these structures until the Spanish conquistadors arrived in the New World in the early 1500s.

How many steps does Quinn the Quail have to climb down before leaving the pyramid? __________

QUAILS

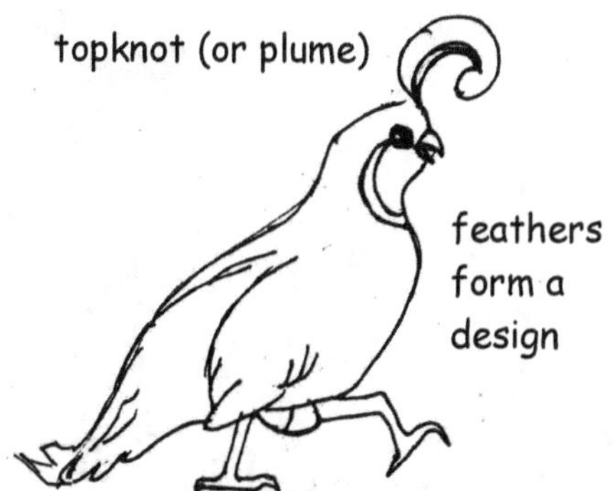

Quails are small, perky birds with funny habits. Most quails have little topknots or plumes, or, as I call them, beeber bobbers, that hang over their small heads, but northern bobwhite quails, like Quinn, actually have rounded crests instead of topknots.

Quails have brown, gray, black, and white feathers; some are specially arranged into patterns that look like scales. Northern bobwhites have black and white heads, and short tails.

Most quails eat small berries, seeds, insects, and plants. When something startles a flock of them, they scatter and burst into flight, but they only stay in the air long enough to find a place to hide. They are short-distance flyers. Quails have to be careful, because animals like cats, foxes, dogs, owls, and even snakes like to eat them. Quails form flocks, or coveys, in the fall, and they lay from ten to twenty eggs at one time. Baby quails are called chicks.

Draw a quail with a stylish topknot.

QUAILS

What do I eat?

What scares me?

What do you like best about me?

How do I protect myself?

RESCUE QUINN FROM A VOLCANO!

Let's take a look inside a volcano.

Here are some parts of the volcano:

Magma–rock that is so hot under the surface of the earth, that it is liquid

Vent–the tunnel-like chamber through which the magma travels out of the volcano, which then turns to lava

Crater–made in the top of the volcano after it erupts and the top blows off

Lava–liquid rock as it flows out of a volcano

Gas–made up of water vapor, sulfur dioxide and other substances, and it escapes when a volcano erupts

Quinn the Quail was careful to avoid any erupting volcanoes as he and the troops traveled to Tenochtitlán, the Aztec capital. The volcano below is about to erupt. Please locate Quinn and draw a circle around him before it does!

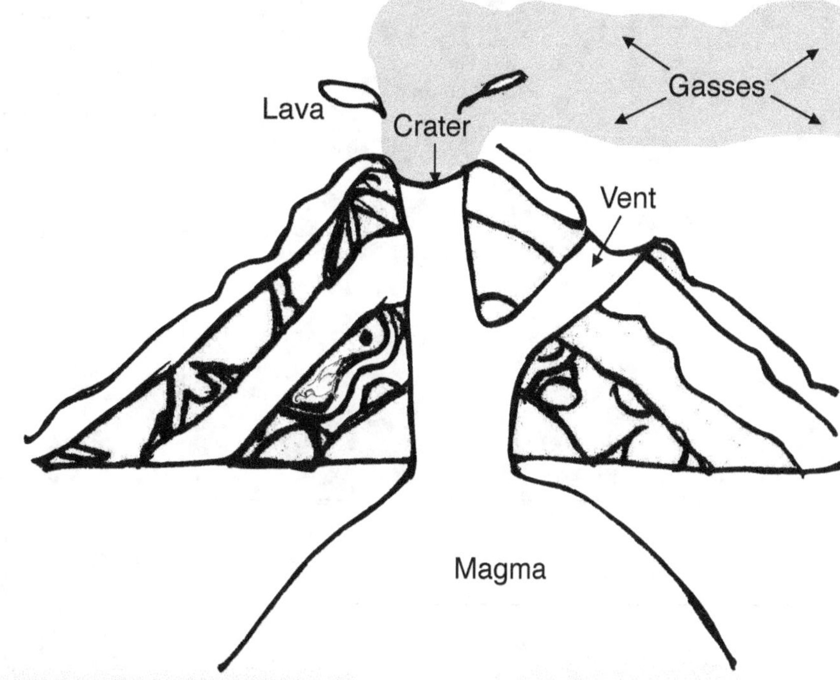

AFRICAN COUNTRIES

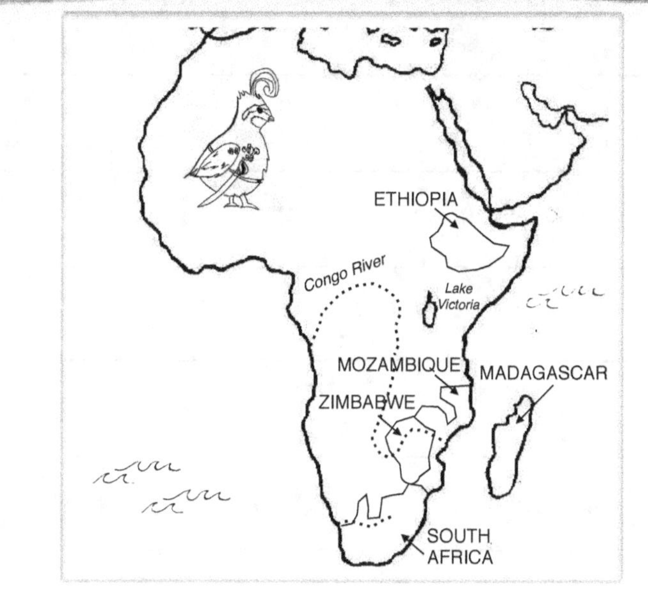

MAP IT!

The Commandment Stone allowed the Animals to travel to some African countries. Color the countries on the map.

1. Color Ethiopia RED.

2. Color Mozambique YELLOW.

3. Color Zimbabwe GREEN.

4. Color Madagascar ORANGE.

5. Color South Africa PURPLE.

ROBERT THE RABBIT

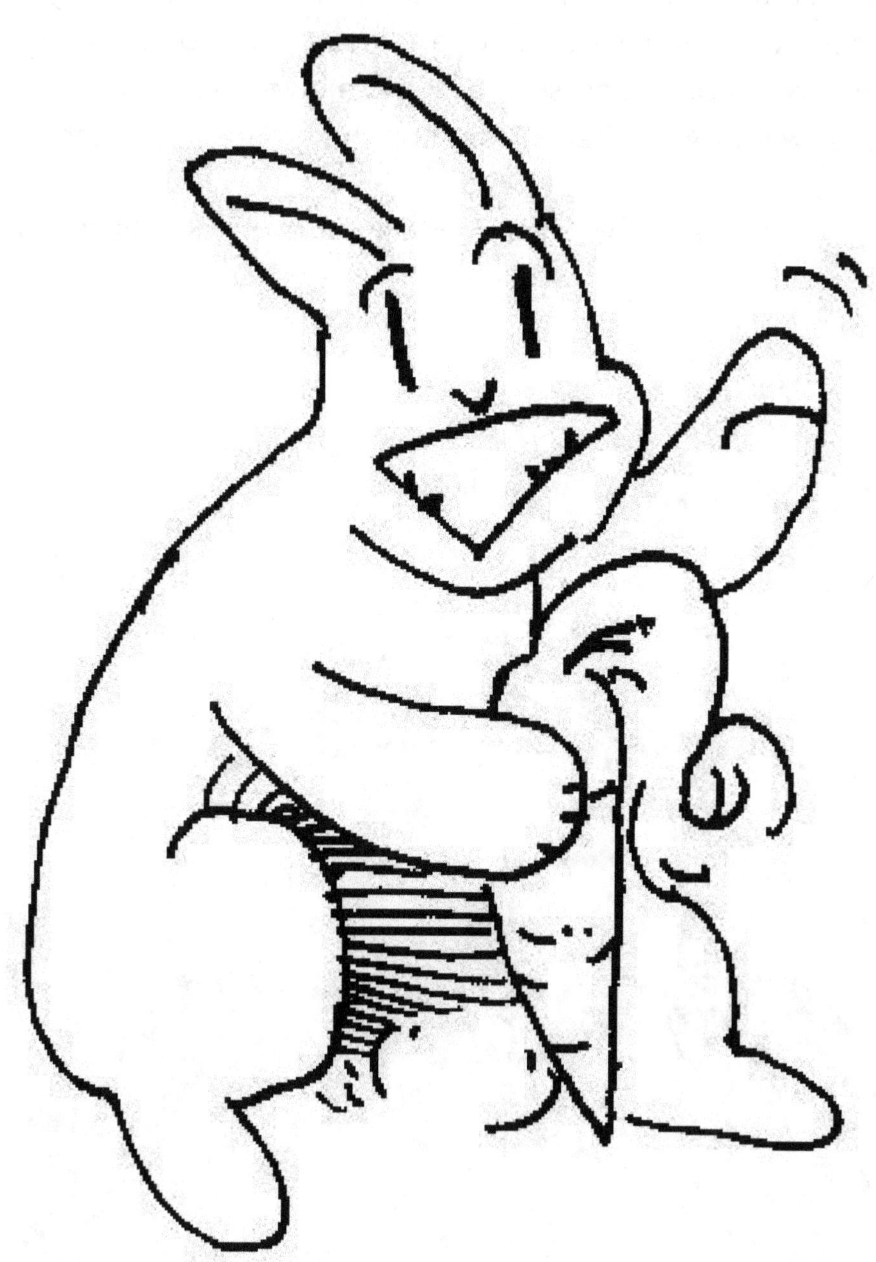

CLIMB A MOUND

Mound-building civilizations in North America, such as the Adena, the Hopewell, and the Mississippians, did not have heavy-duty construction vehicles we use today to build. They used their hands and backs to make their mounds, layering soil, clay, and stones. There were often steps on one side and a hut on top where a ruler lived. The mounds had many purposes, such as temple ceremonies and burial sites. Also, when the floods swept by, the items in and on the mound were safe.

In the mound below, draw some important items of yours that you would like to keep safe.

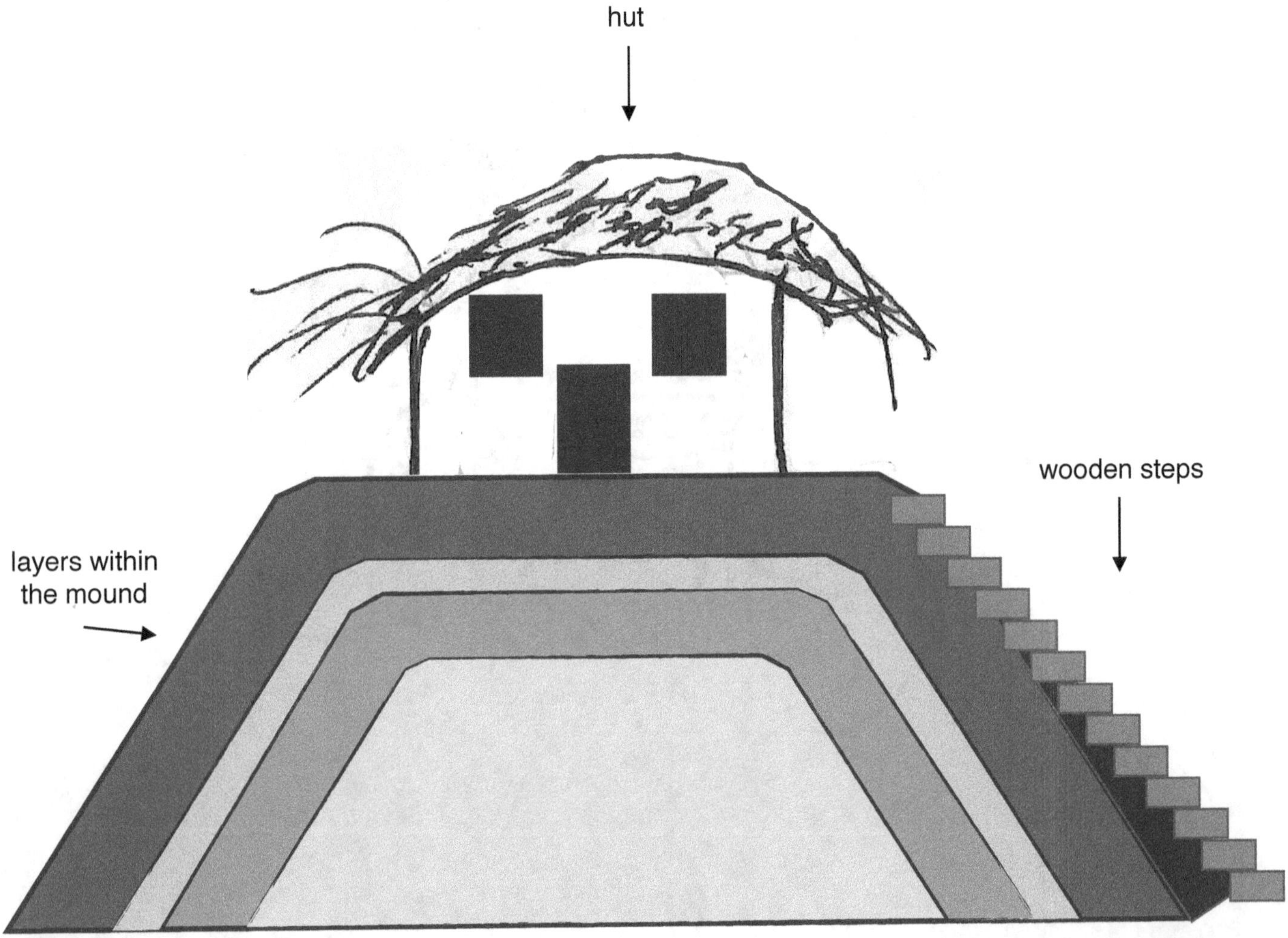

RABBITS

Rabbits are little creatures with big ears, twitchy noses, and fast legs. They are usually very quiet and cautious because so many things like to eat them. It's a real treat if you get to see a rabbit out in the open.

Rabbits stay together in groups. In some groups of rabbits, the mommies, or does, all have babies at around the same time. Rabbits have lots of babies, called kits or kittens. They have up to six at once. These babies are born without fur, and they cannot open their eyes for a few days. But when they do, they sure are hungry!

All rabbits eat plants. Swamp rabbits, like Robert, live in wet areas, so they eat plants that grow there: bark, seeds, grasses, and even twigs. They mostly eat at night, when they have less chance of being eaten themselves. These rabbits also like to swim, and they go to the water to escape predators, just like Robert escaped the kite in the story. Other than kites, there are many other animals that like to have rabbits for their breakfast, including birds, wild cats, dogs, snakes, and water predators like alligators. That's why rabbits have to be quick and hard to catch.

Draw a feast on the plate below that a swamp rabbit would enjoy!

RABBITS

R4

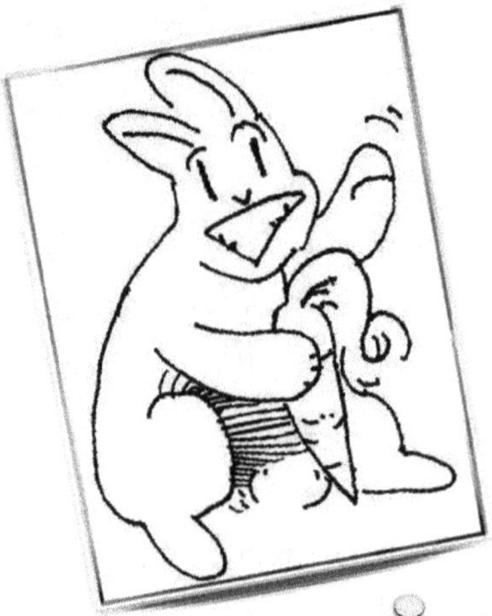

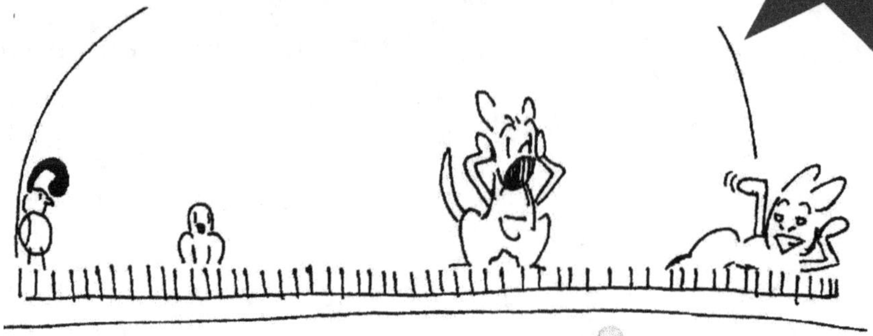

What do I eat?

What scares me?

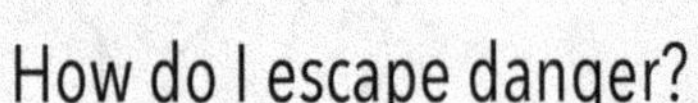

What do you like best about me?

How do I escape danger?

SWEPT AWAY INTO AN OCEAN TRENCH

Have you ever seen a mountain? How about a hill? Of course you have! How about a canyon like the Grand Canyon? Well, there are mountains and canyons and more in the ocean too.

When a flash flood swept past the Animals, the Commandment Stone harnesses got swept downriver too. They eventually made it to the sea. Draw a path showing them traveling from the continental shelf to the abyssal plain over the mid-ocean ridge and down into the trench.

Here are some types of ocean floor:

Continental shelf–the slope from the area you call beach until where the slope becomes very steep

Abyssal plain–flat areas in the deep ocean floor

Mid-ocean ridge–mountain ranges in the sea

Trench–deepest parts of the ocean

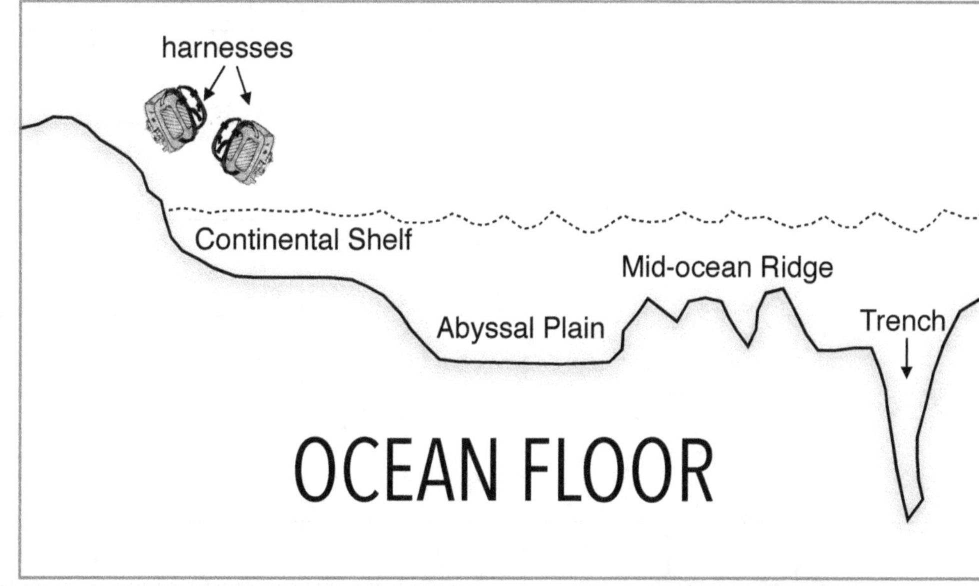

MESOAMERICA REGIONS

MAP IT!

After exploring regions in Mesoamerica, Amber and the others decided to tour North America. Color the Mesoamerican regions they visited.

1. Color the Gulf of Mexico BLUE.

2. Circle the Yucatan Peninsula in RED.

3. Color the Aztec Civilization GREEN.

4. Color the Olmec Civilization PINK.

5. Color the Maya Civilization ORANGE.

R6

SAMMY THE SQUIRREL

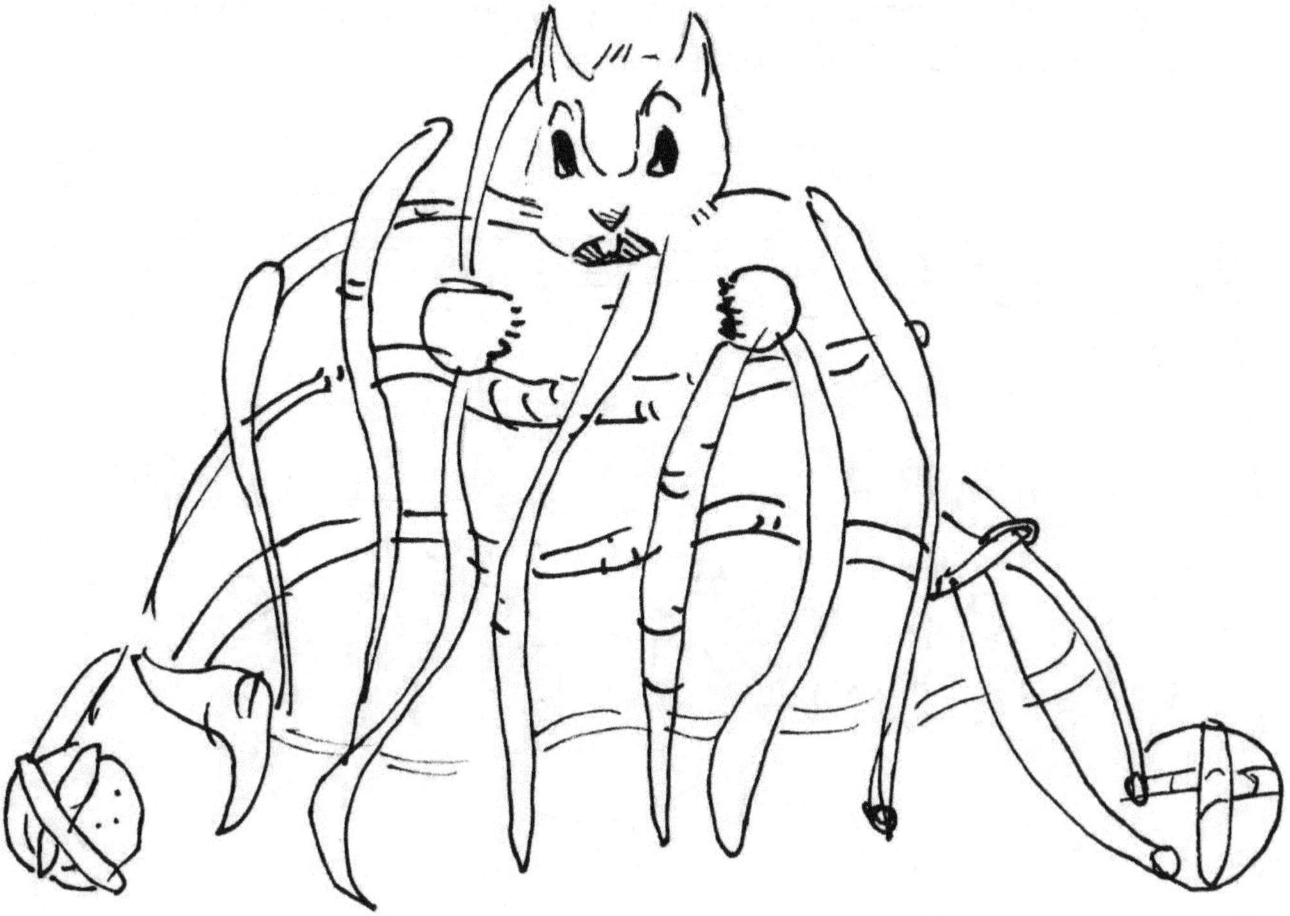

HOMES IN THE ROCKS

Many years ago, there were people who were very good at making baskets, sandals, cord, and pottery. They were the Ancestral Pueblo people, also called the Anasazi, and they lived in the southwestern corner of what we now call the United States. While they once lived in pits—holes in the ground covered with a roof of branches and mud—they eventually began to build homes above the ground. Using stone, they constructed impressive homes on rock ledges, called cliff dwellings. In order to get to their homes in the rocks, they usually had to climb up, using ropes or ladders.

If you lived in the cliff dwellings below, how would you choose to climb up to your house? Draw your answer below, and then color the rocks and homes.

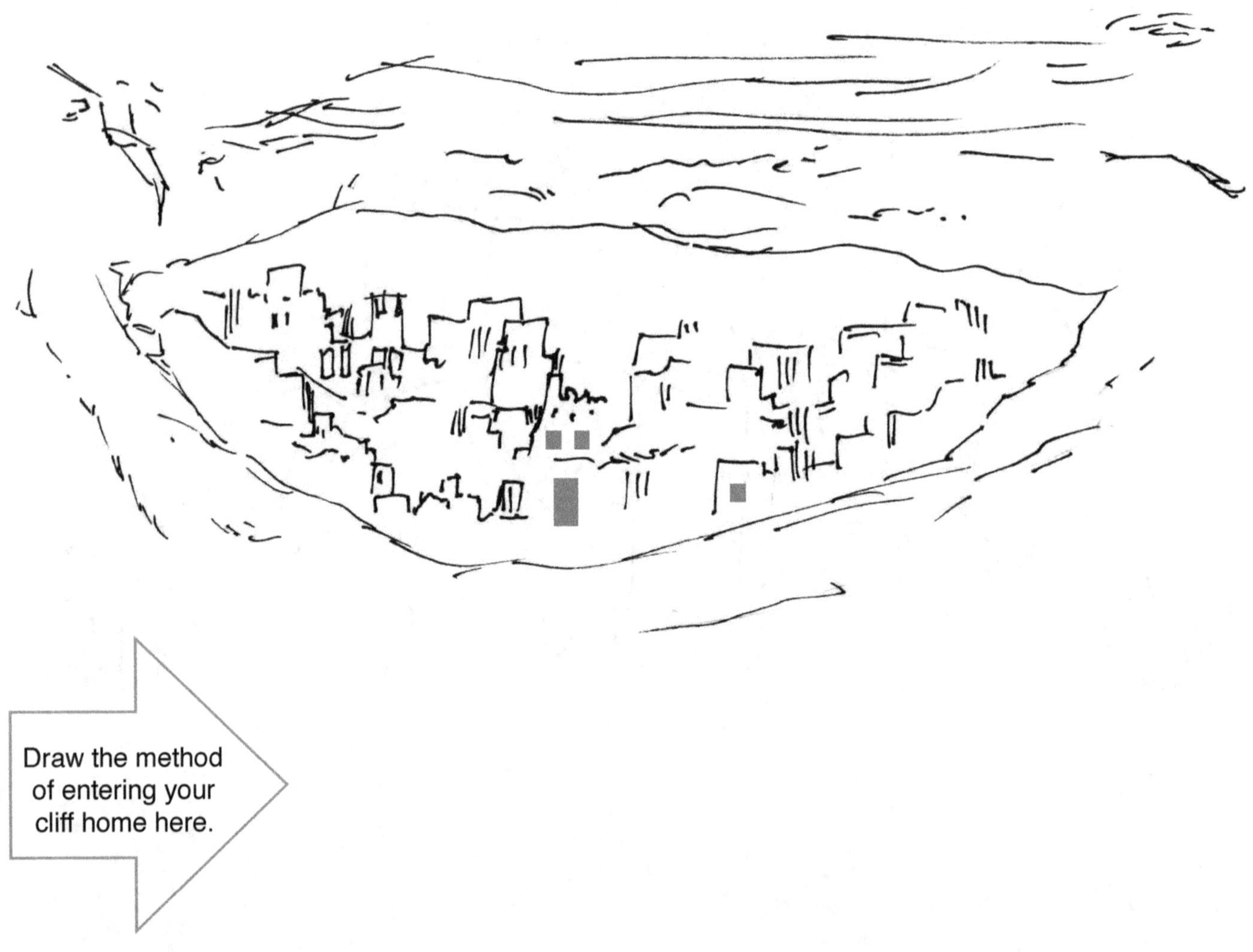

Draw the method of entering your cliff home here.

SQUIRRELS

Chattering noises up in the trees often come from squirrels—climbing, mousey-like creatures with small ears and big tails. American red squirrels, like Sammy, are smaller than most and have less bushy tails. Sammy probably used his small size in getting away from the Anasazi.

The name squirrel can mean "shadow tail," and they sure are quick and fast. If a predator like a fierce bird or a snake tries to catch them, they can bounce around in different directions to confuse the predator, before dashing up into a tree. Squirrels have special toes with sharp claws and double-jointed hind legs, which help them climb trees. Because they're so jumpy, squirrels have to eat a lot of nuts, fruits, seeds, and bugs to give them energy. Their front teeth never stop growing!

American red squirrels are very protective, and they don't like to share their tree trunk nests, called dreys. They keep their babies, or kittens, safe, because, like rabbits, they are born blind. They depend on their mothers until they are old enough to go and tease some humans on their own!

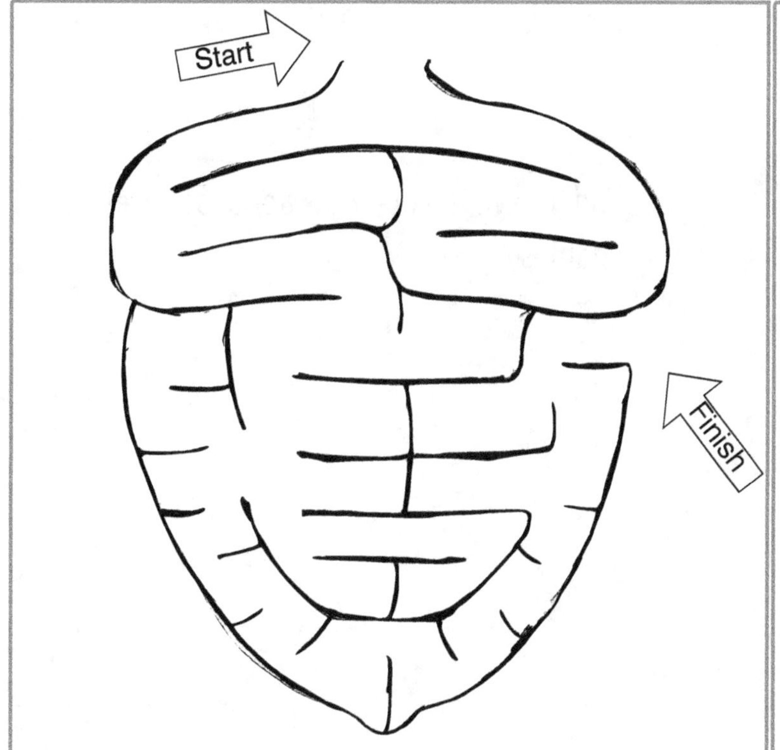

Draw an acorn with a unique design on it.

SQUIRRELS

S4

What do I eat?

What scares me, and what do I do to escape?

What do you like best about me?

Tell me what you know about squirrel babies.

OCEAN ZONES: HOW LOW CAN YOU GO?

Have you ever eaten a cake with different layers? What are your favorite flavors? Well, the ocean is also divided into different layers, although you couldn't eat these layers.

Here are some of the layers, or zones, of the ocean:

Epipelagic–the surface layer of the ocean, also known as the sunlight zone

Mesopelagic–also known as the twilight zone because the light it receives is very faint

Bathypelagic–the dark zone, also known as the midnight zone

Abyssalpelagic–known as the abyss; there's no light here and the temperature is near freezing

Color the zone known as the sunlight zone ORANGE.
Color the twilight zone GREEN.
Color the midnight zone BLUE.
Color the abyss PURPLE.
Now, draw yourself in the zone where you would swim.

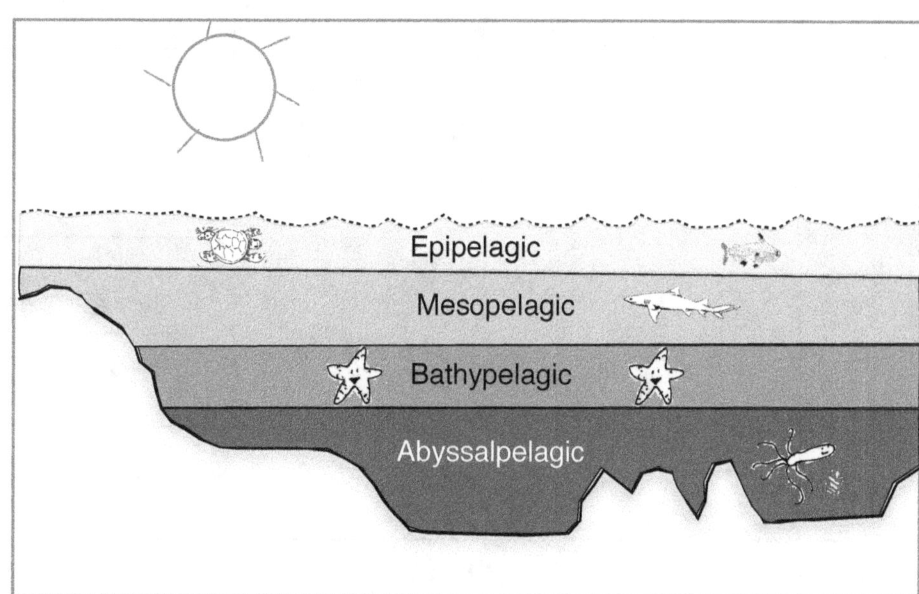

MESOAMERICA

MAP IT!

The Commandment Stone allowed the Animals to travel to some African countries. Color the countries on the map.

1. Color Lake Texcoco BLUE.

2. Circle Mexico City in RED.

3. Circle Mayapan in GREEN.

4. Circle Chichen Itza in ORANGE.

5. Circle Oaxaca in PURPLE.

S6

TABOR THE TURTLE

GUN POWDER IN MEXICO

President Díaz wanted to turn his country of Mexico into a modern place with roads and factories. It was a good idea, but he was a dictator: he ruled by trying to control everyone, including forcing the people off of their farms to use the land for other things. This caused people to fight back, which was one of the reasons that the Mexican Revolution began. Men like Pancho Villa and Emiliano Zapata fought for "Land and Liberty." But it wasn't only men who fought. Women also joined them in the fighting. They were called soldaderas—women soldiers.

Here are two things to do on the map below.
1. Draw a line from the earliest battle shown on the map to the following battles, in order of dates.
2. Circle the battle that erupted near Tabor the Turtle's home.

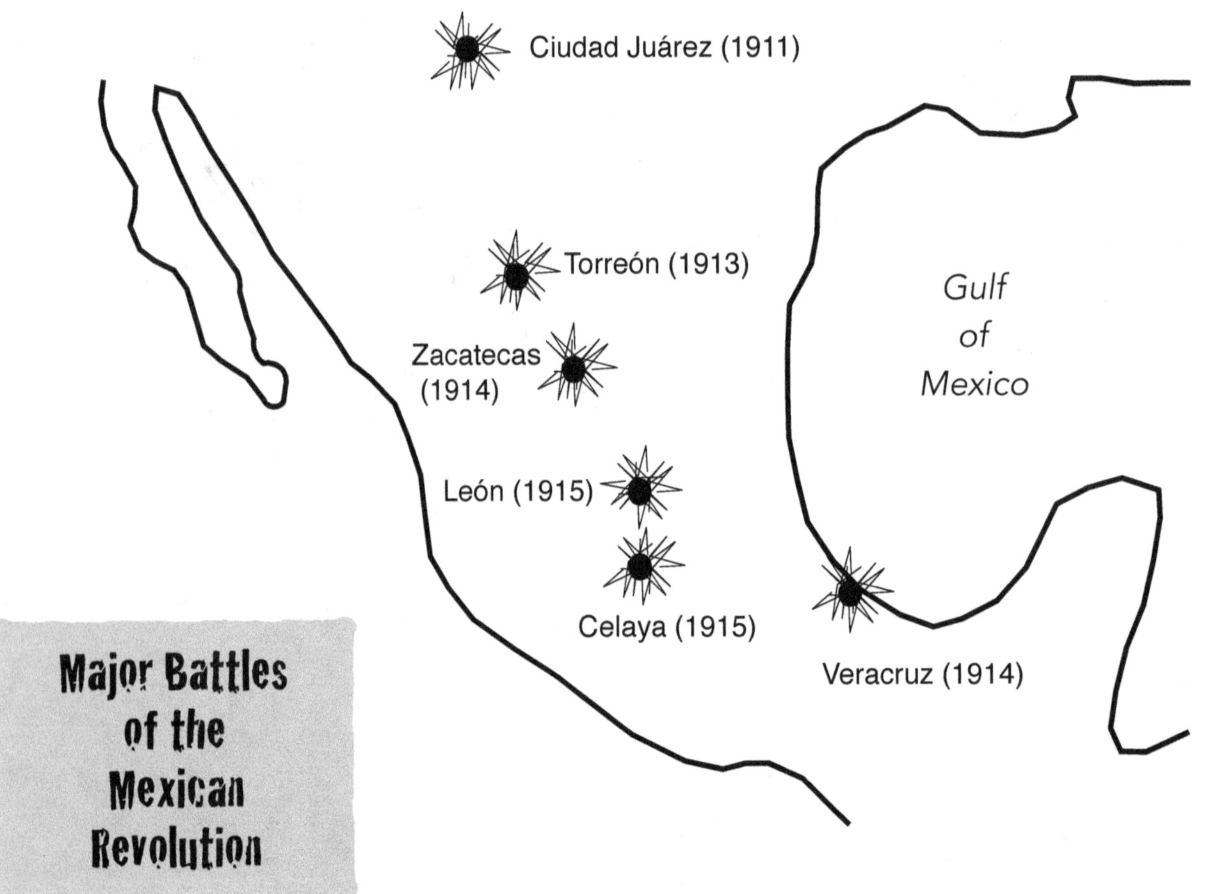

TURTLES

You can recognize a turtle by its large, hard shell covering its back. This shell is called a carapace, and it protects the turtle and helps it glide through the water. However, other animals still like to eat them, so turtles must have other ways to protect themselves.

Tabor is a hawksbill turtle, a kind of sea turtle that uses its sharp beak to snag delicious sponges out of rocks. Jellyfish, mollusks, and sea urchins are also tasty treats. Hawksbill turtles have overlapping plates that look like spikes at the edges of their heart-shaped shells. From the way they look, you wouldn't want to bother a hawksbill!

Sadly, there are not many hawksbill turtles left. It's important for them to lay their eggs safely so they aren't eaten by wild animals and other predators. If startled, a mother Hawksbill can stand on her flippers and run away, a little like an alligator. She'll lay over fifty eggs in a nest made out of sand on a beautiful beach, then she will go back to the water. When the eggs hatch, the little turtles have to scramble for their lives across the sand to the sea before a seagull or a crab gets them!

Ever tasted seawater? Bleck! It's salty! But sea turtles have parts of their bodies that filter the salt out of the water they drink. Because of this, turtles like Tabor can have all the fun they want in the sea without worrying about the salt!

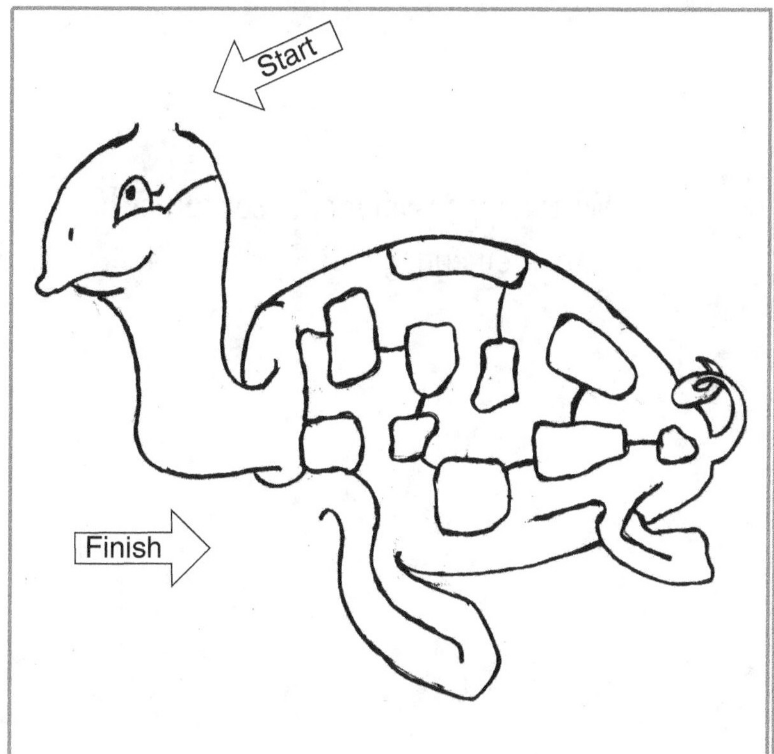

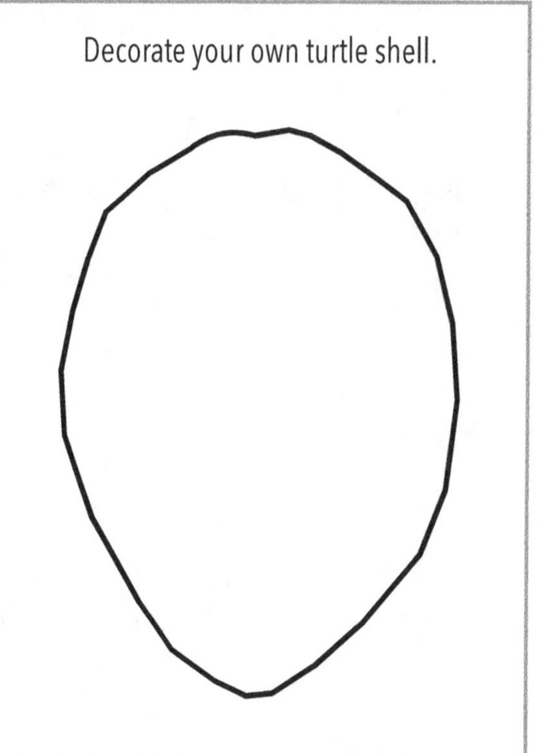

Decorate your own turtle shell.

TURTLES

T4

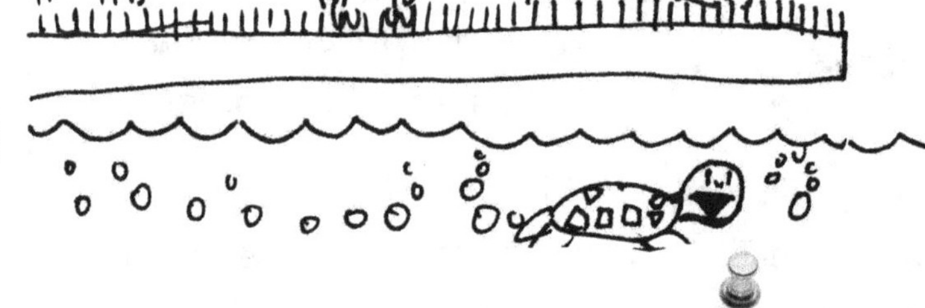

What do I eat?

What is special about the way I drink water?

What do you like best about me?

What happens after baby sea turtles hatch from their eggs?

BLANKETS AROUND PLANET EARTH

Have you ever crawled under a big pile of blankets? Imagine you pulled five blankets over you. That's a little like what parts of the atmosphere around our planet are like. The atmosphere is made up of gasses that protect Earth.

Here are some of the parts of the atmosphere:

Exosphere–the outermost and thinnest layer

Thermosphere–can get very hot because the air is very thin

Mesosphere–the coldest layer; where meteors burn up

Stratosphere–heated from the sun; weather balloons can go this high

Troposphere–the layer covering the surface of the Earth and is heated by the earth; this is where we live and where airplanes fly

Draw yourself and your family in the part of the atmosphere where you would be most comfortable.

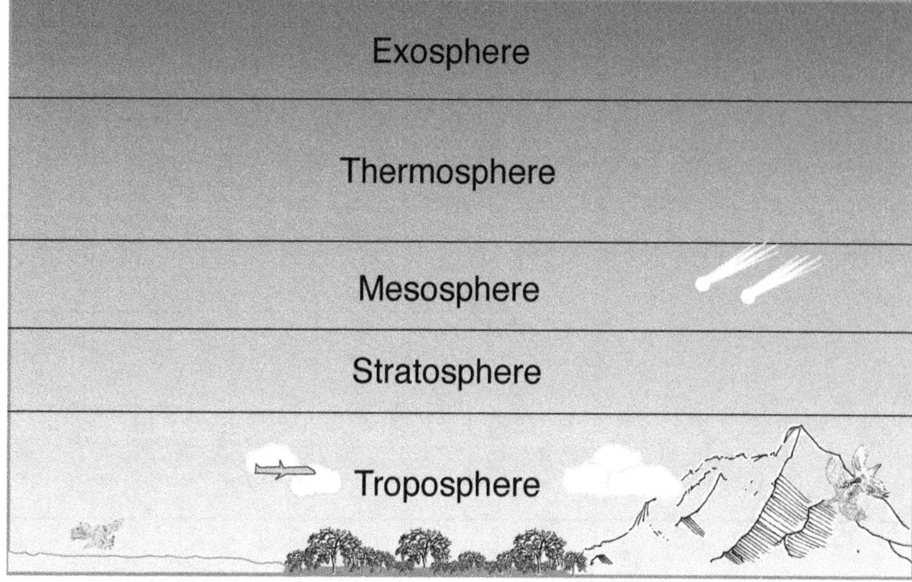

DOMINION OF CANADA

MAP IT!

Tabor the Turtle could swim far, but he preferred warmer waters. Color the locations below that were too cold for him.

1. Color Quebec GREEN.

2. Color Ontario ORANGE.

3. Color New Brunswick RED.

4. Color Nova Scotia YELLOW.

URIAH THE URIAL

MAPLE LEAVES IN CANADA

Canada is a country in North America, and it is very large. The only country bigger than Canada is Russia. There is a river in Canada called the St. Lawrence River, or St. Lawrence Seaway, that allows people to move important goods from one country to another on boat. Some of these goods are salt, stone, and iron ore—the main material used in steel. The St. Lawrence River was explored by John Cabot, who first set sail from Europe in 1497, on a voyage to Asia. Instead of finding Asia, however, he ran into an island off the coast of North America. Years later, in 1603, another explorer named Samuel de Champlain sailed from France to North America. He navigated through the river and made maps that helped ships sail from the Great Lakes to the Atlantic Ocean.

The maple leaf is the symbol of Canada. Help Uriah the Urial and Samuel de Champlain locate the maple leaves in the picture below, and then circle or color them. When the maple leaves have been spotted, Uriah will know he is near Canada.

maple leaf

URIALS

horns that point back toward neck, point forward, or point in different directions

hooves

Chances are, you've never seen a urial before. This kind of mountain sheep lives in southern Asia, and it likes high, grassy areas. Urials look a little like antelopes, with their long legs, large, curved horns, and wiry bodies.

Urials have long, reddish-brown hair with a large, white patch on their hind legs. They recognize each other by smell and live in groups, except when a mommy has a baby. These sheep are quick and excellent climbers, but they have to watch out for wild dogs, large cats, and eagles.

Urials like to eat grasses and grain, although Uriah would of course prefer a barrel of maple syrup to a bunch of dry shrubs. They can be aggressive and will fight with each other. However, urials are considered vulnerable, and they have to be protected so that they do not die out.

Urials have horns in the shape of spirals. Fill this box with either one giant spiral or many small spirals.

URIALS

U4

What do I eat?

What scares me?

What do you like best about me?

How would you describe the way I look?

RINGS AROUND THE WORLD

Without maps, we would wander around, not sure where to go. Even without a map on paper or a navigation system, like on a phone or in a car, we still make points in our mind about where things are. For example, when you drive somewhere in town, you have reference points such as a specific gas station or restaurant that you look for to know when it's time to turn. Well, there are reference points on our planet as well that are actually imaginary lines.

There are five imaginary lines, or circles of latitude:

Arctic Circle
Tropic of Cancer
Equator
Tropic of Capricorn
Antarctic Circle

➤ **When Uriah the Urial wanted to figure out how much maple syrup was left in his barrel, he would measure based on his own circles of latitude. When the syrup was filled to the top, it was at the Arctic Circle line, but when it was almost gone, the syrup was far down at the Antarctic Circle. Trace over each of the lines on the earth below in different colors, and then circle each circle of latitude on the left in the color that matches the ones on the earth.**

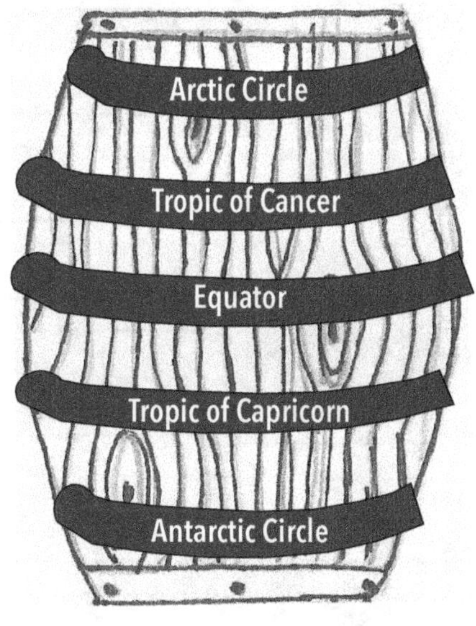

CANADIAN WATERS

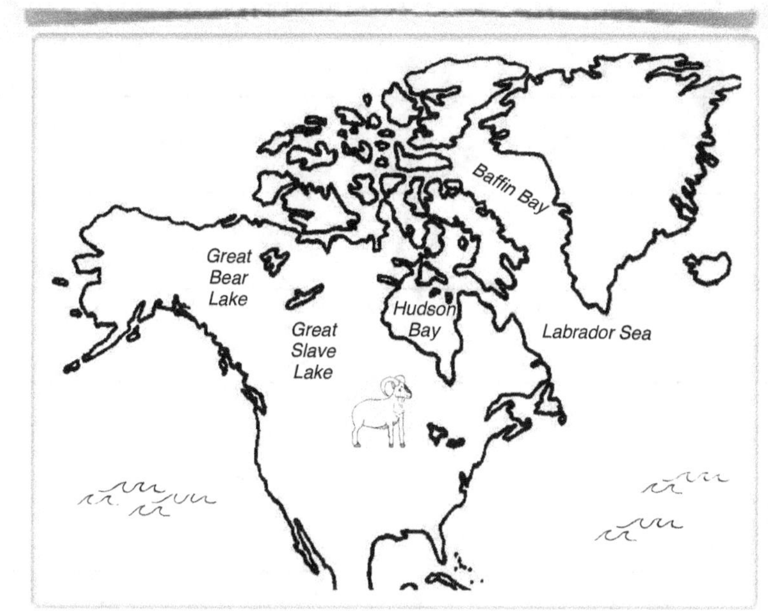

MAP IT!

After exploring regions in Mesoamerica, Amber and the others decided to tour North America. Color the Mesoamerican regions they visited.

1. Color the Baffin Bay BLUE.

2. Circle the Labrador Sea in RED.

3. Color the Hudson Bay GREEN.

4. Color the Great Bear Lake PINK.

5. Color the Great Slave Lake ORANGE.

U6

VIVIEN THE VULTURE

MAKE A CAKE FOR CANADA

Most people love a birthday party! It's a time to celebrate a person, and what better day than the day they were born. While it's easy to associate a person with a specific day of birth, it's not always as clear with the birth of a country. This is the case with Canada. After the American Civil War, the Canadians worried the victorious Americans in the North would also want to take Canada, so they decided to make themselves stronger by pulling the different provinces together—the British North America Act united New Brunswick, Nova Scotia, Quebec, and Ontario into the Dominion of Canada. This happened on July 1, 1867, which is why they celebrate Canada's birthday every July 1st.
Note: It wasn't until 1982 that Canadians gained complete independence from Britain.

It's time to light the candles and decorate a cake! Add some flames to the candles, write the date of Canada's birthday on the line below the maple leaf, and then add decorations anywhere you want to make the wildest cake you can think of.

VULTURES

Vultures might not look pretty, but they get the job done. These birds have all the tools they need to do their natural jobs. Not all vultures have such beautiful names as Vivien, but they have some pretty impressive features.

Vultures are large birds with powerful wings. Turkey vultures, like Vivien, have a layer of brownish-black flight feathers covering some beautiful silvery-gray plumage underneath. Their heads might look like a turkey's, but they sure aren't. Unlike other birds, vultures have an amazing sense of smell, thanks to their great noses. You can see right through a turkey vulture's nose. They use their sniffers to find fresh meat.

Vulture eggs are laid right on the ground, or inside trees or rocks, without a nest! They are creamy white, with dark brown markings. Vivien's egg had a special marking of a maple leaf. The eggs are kept warm by both the mom and dad, and when the babies hatch, the parents take turns feeding and watching over them. If the babies are surprised without a parent guarding them, they will hiss and spit, scaring the predator away. Don't mess with them!

Draw an egg for each child in your family and decorate each with unique markings.

VULTURES

Tell me about my sense of smell.

How do we parent vultures take care of our eggs before they hatch?

What do you like best about me?

How do we protect ourselves when we are still babies?

DANCES AND BATTLES IN THE AIR

Do you know what air is? You might say it's something you breathe, and that is correct! Air is inside of us and all around us. It is a mixture of gasses (mostly nitrogen and oxygen), and it makes up the Earth's atmosphere.

An air mass is a big bunch of air that has the same temperature and amount of moisture. When two air masses, or big bunches of air, meet it's called a front. The two air masses don't mix. It's a dance and sometimes a battle between warm and cold air, sometimes pushing under, sliding over, trapping in between, or standing still because neither can move.

Our weather, sometimes calm, other times stormy, happens based on the dances and battles in the air. So when the rain and snow fall, or the wind races around you, you know there's a dance taking place in the air.

Vivien is a weather tracker, and sometimes she makes sketches of the weather patterns on the tree branch where she sleeps. You may see symbols like these on the weather station on TV. Follow the directions for each of the weather fronts below.

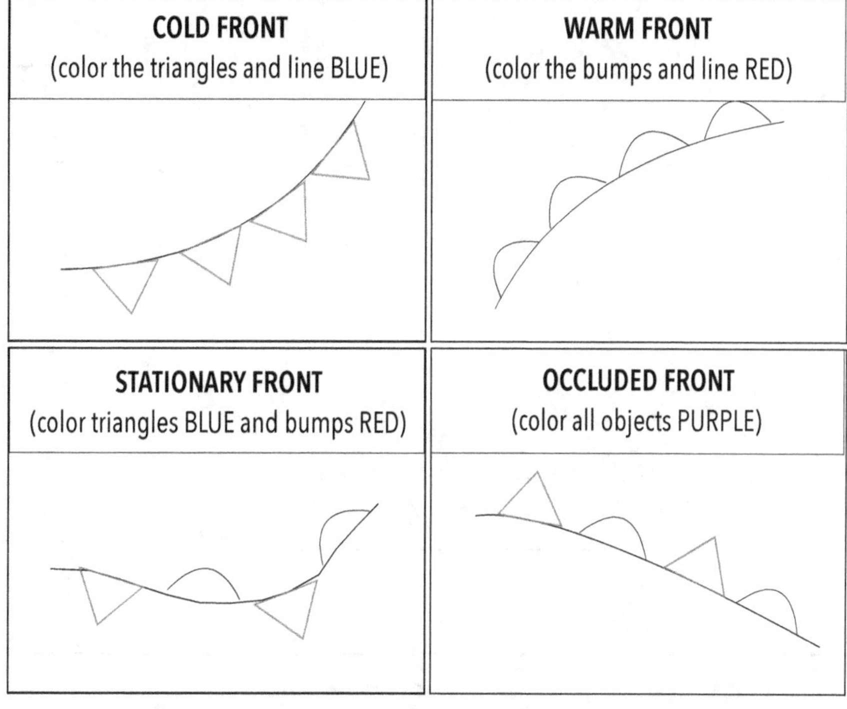

SOUTH AMERICA (WEST)

MAP IT!

While exploring countries in South America, a thief stole the Commandment Stone. Color the South American countries they visited.

1. Color Venezuela RED.

2. Color Colombia ORANGE.

3. Color Ecuador YELLOW.

4. Color Peru GREEN.

5. Color Bolivia BLUE.

6. Color Chile PURPLE.

V6

WILLIAM THE WOLF

SOUTH AMERICA IS LIBERATED

After Quinn the Quail marched through South America with Spanish Conquistador Cortés and captured the Aztec Empire in the early 1500s, Spain and Portugal eventually ended up colonizing most of South America. Three hundred years later, in the 1800s, South America was liberated, with the help of José de San Martín, Bernardo O'Higgins, and Simón Bolívar.

Draw a line from each of the men below to their countries in South America. You may need a map to help you.

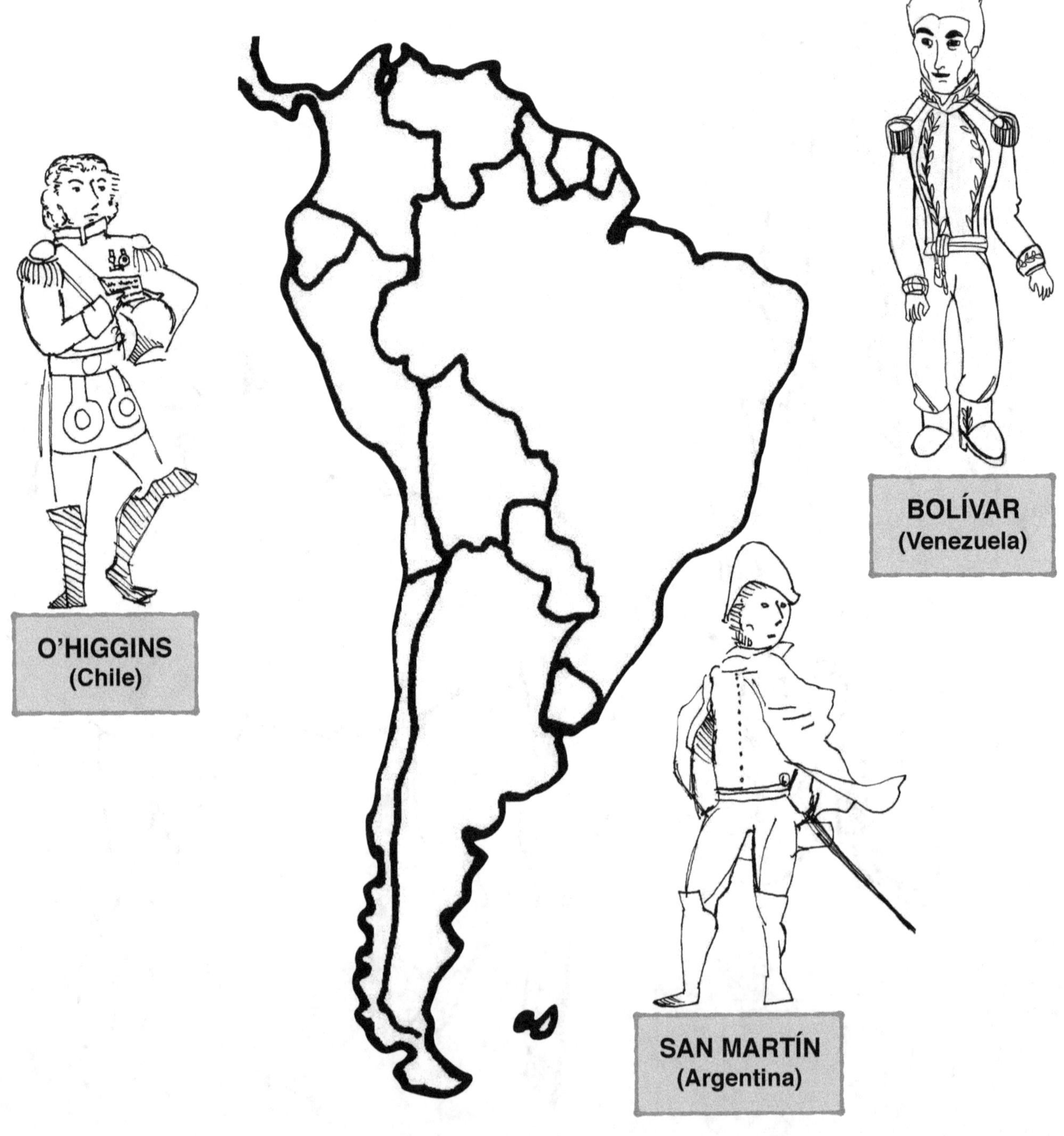

MANED WOLVES

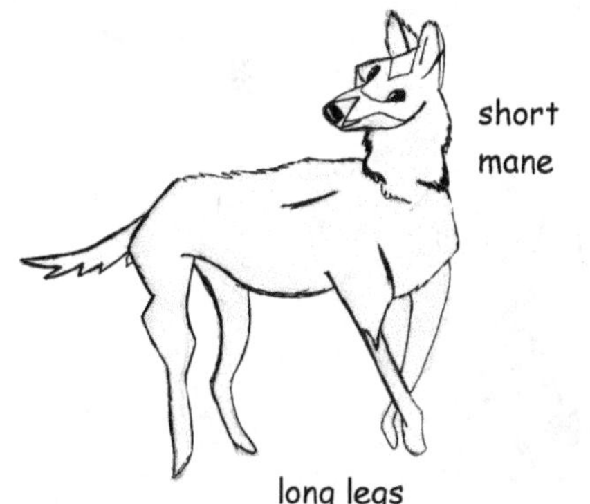

Wolves are fierce, powerful creatures, known to be able to run for long periods of time, and to use teamwork to take down the toughest prey. Maned wolves, like William, may be in the Canid family with wolves, foxes, and dogs, but they are in a genus group of their own. They're something very special.

Maned wolves are golden-red, dog-like creatures, named for a bunch of fur called a mane that stands up when they are surprised or angry. Even with the mane, they are not related to lions, but to dogs, wolves, and foxes. Maned wolves have very long and skinny legs, which help them run fast through the long grass of their home. They have to be quick to be able to catch rabbits and rodents. Maned wolves have small jaws and, therefore, eat small prey and lobeira fruit, something like a tomato. Maned wolf pups have to eat a lot to grow big and strong and have pups of their own.

These creatures like living in open grasslands near the edges of forests. When a maned wolf pup is born, both parents care for it, feed it, and groom it. After a year, they're ready to go off on their own. Maned wolves hunt when it's dark, and they spend the day resting under bushes.

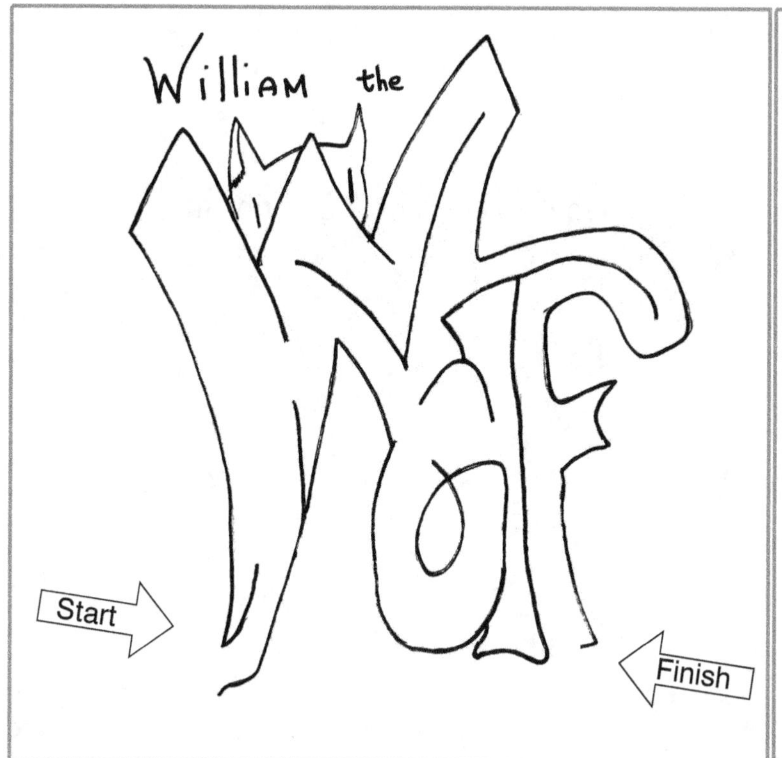

This is the shape of an lobeira fruit, a favorite treat of maned wolves. Fill the platter below with as many of these fruits as you think William the Wolf would like to eat.

WOLVES

What other animals are we related to?

How do we parent maned wolves take care of our young?

What do you like best about me?

What do I look like? Describe me.

HELD HOSTAGE IN THE CLOUDS

We have already learned about air, but do you know what a cloud floating in the air is? Try to describe it. Would you say it's a white puffy thing in the sky? Well, clouds are actually big bunches, or masses, of waterdrops or ice crystals floating in the sky.

Here are some types of clouds:

Cumulonimbus–at all levels in the sky, can exist as a single tower or can form a line of towers, can make hail, lighting, thunderstorms, and tornadoes

Cirrus–high in the sky, look like wispy curls of hair, and whiter than other types

Stratus–low to the ground and can become fog, look like a sheet or blanket in the sky

Cumulus–big, puffy clouds that look like cauliflower or heaps of mashed potatoes; perfect for skywatching on a sunny day

Stratocumulus–low-level and a mix of stratus and cumulus, so they are like sheets of heaps

Vorus and his buzzard cohorts captured the Animals in a net. Write the type of cloud on the lines provided, and then draw a line showing the buzzards' path through the clouds in this order:
1. Cumulonimbus 2. Cirrus 3. Cumulus
4. Stratocumulus 5. Stratus

SOUTH AMERICA (EAST)

MAP IT!

The buzzard wanted to send the Animals to a country in South America. Color the countries he considered sending them.

1. Color Argentina PINK.

2. Color Uruguay GRAY.

3. Color Paraguay LIGHT BLUE.

4. Color Brazil LIGHT GREEN.

5. Color French Guiana TAN.

6. Color Suriname LAVENDER.

7. Color Guyana BLACK.

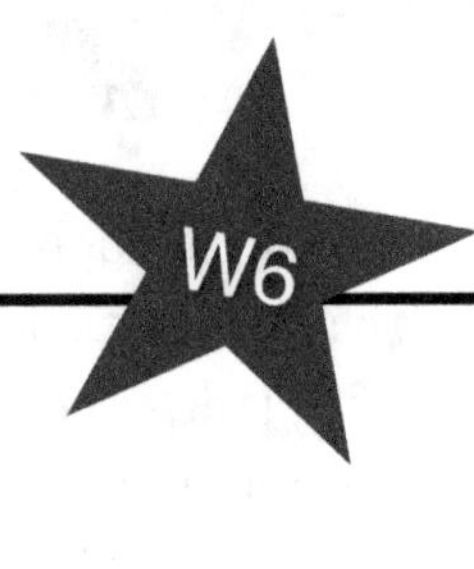

W6

XANDE THE X-RAY TETRA

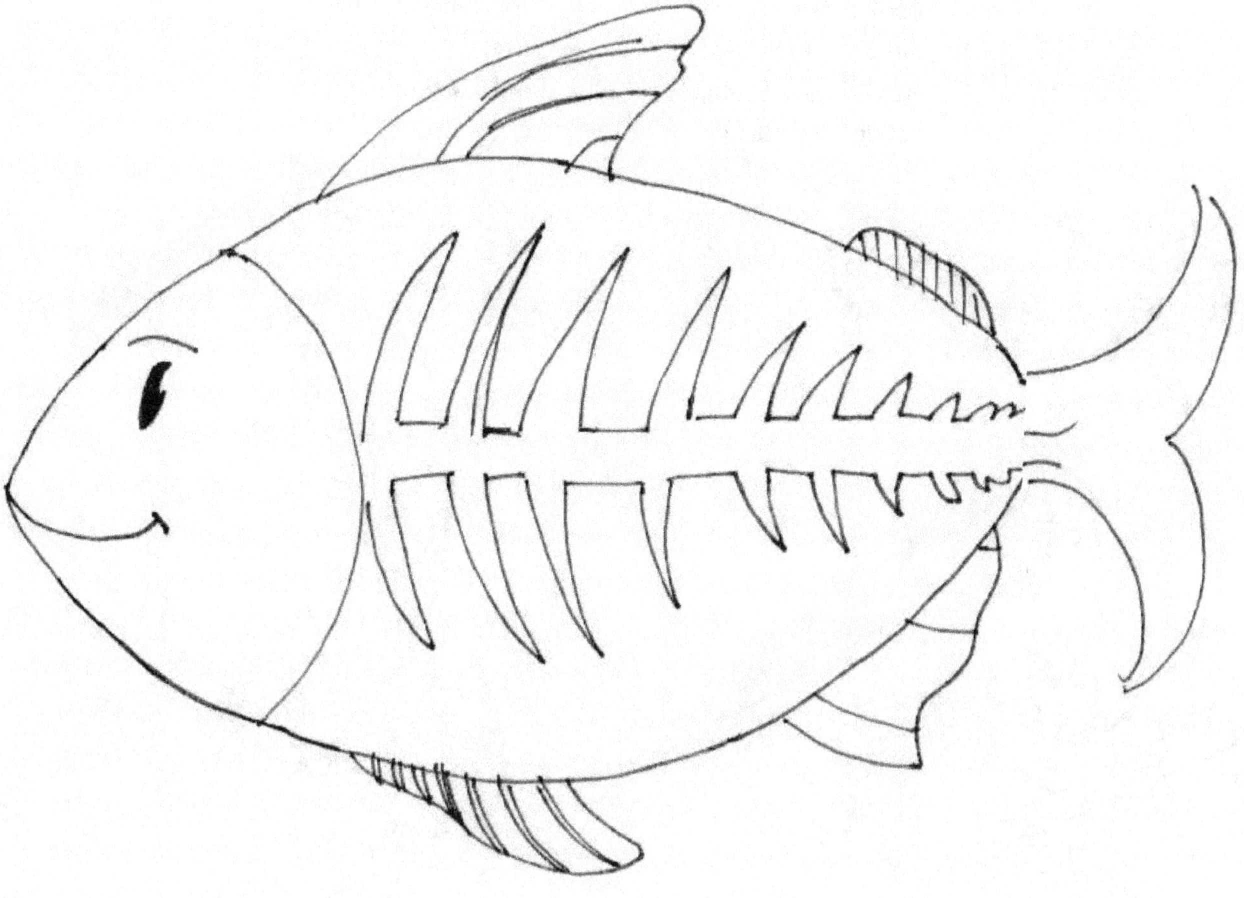

DOM PEDRO AND A LITTLE FISH

Xande the X-Ray Tetra was friends with Dom Pedro I of Portugal. Dom Pedro had moved to Brazil with his father, King John VI, when they escaped Napoleon's invasion. Brazil was controlled by Portugal at this time, but Dom Pedro I eventually freed Brazil from Portugal's grip. He was known as "the Liberator" and announced, "Hail to the independence, to freedom, and to the separation of Brazil. For my blood, my honor, my God, I swear to give Brazil freedom. Independence or death!"

Xande is a good swimmer. He prefers warmer temperatures, but today he plans to visit some faraway places. He is starting from his home in Brazil and swimming to Africa. Draw the path of Xande's journey from each of the points below. (The first part of his swim has been drawn for you.)

1. Brazil to Africa
2. Africa to Puerto Rico
3. Puerto Rico to Portugal
4. Portugal to Iceland
5. Iceland to Greenland
6. Greenland to Cuba
7. Cuba to Brazil

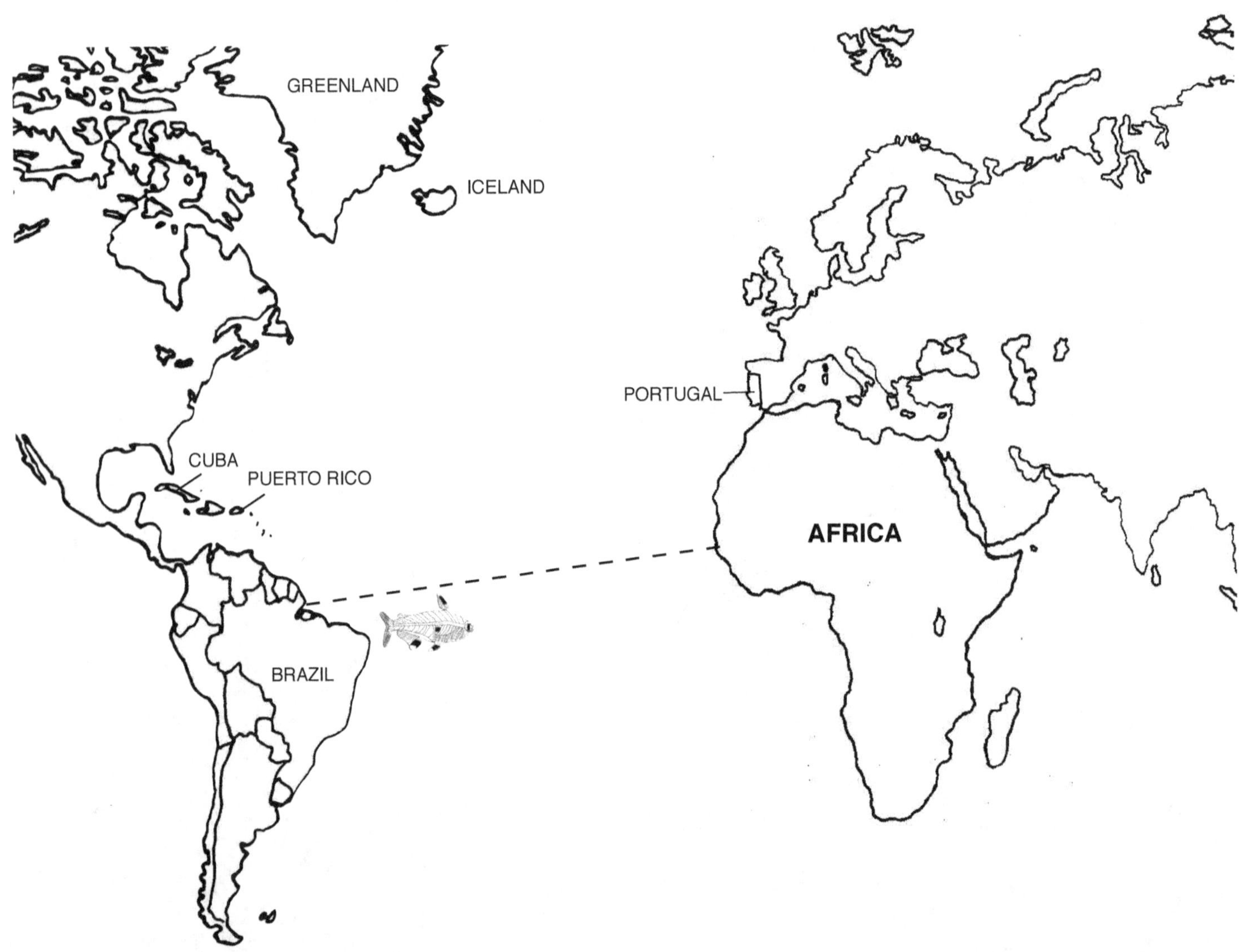

X-RAY TETRA

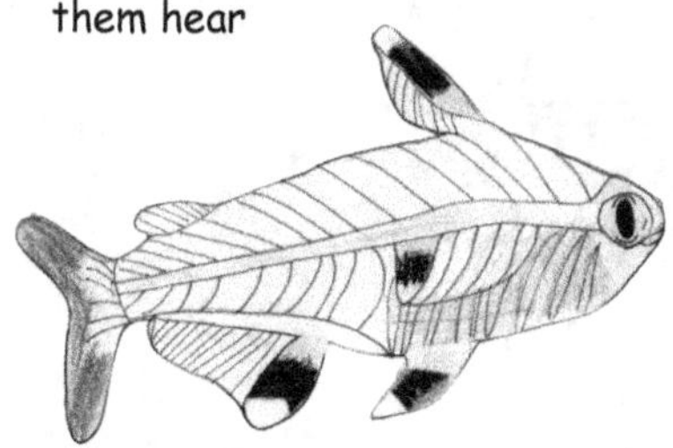

bony internal structure which picks up sound waves and helps them hear

X-ray tetras can be hard to spot. That's because you can see what's on the other side of them! These fishes' bodies are almost completely transparent, except for their bones. The x-ray tetra is also called the golden pristella tetra because of its faint golden color. Xande would like that.

X-ray tetras lay a lot of eggs at one time. About 400! When hatchlings emerge, they are called frys, and they can begin swimming very soon after they hatch.

X-ray tetras are very good at sharing their homes with other animals. They are peaceful fish. They love to munch on worms and insects, and they have excellent hearing, which helps them catch their food. However, they need to watch out for their own predators too, such as snakes or bigger fish. Their clear bodies match the shimmering water, so they can make a quick getaway.

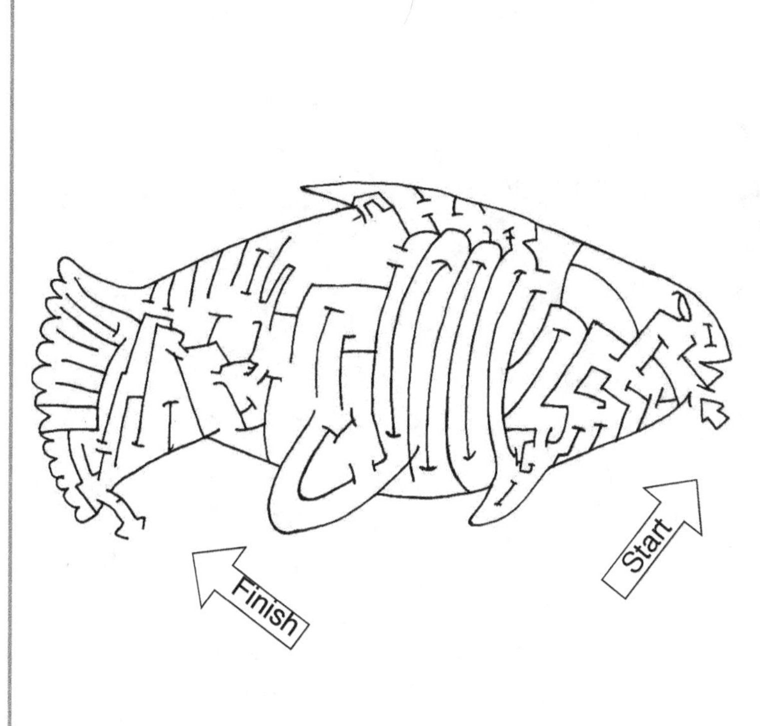

Draw an x-ray tetra with as many eggs as you can.

X-RAY TETRAS

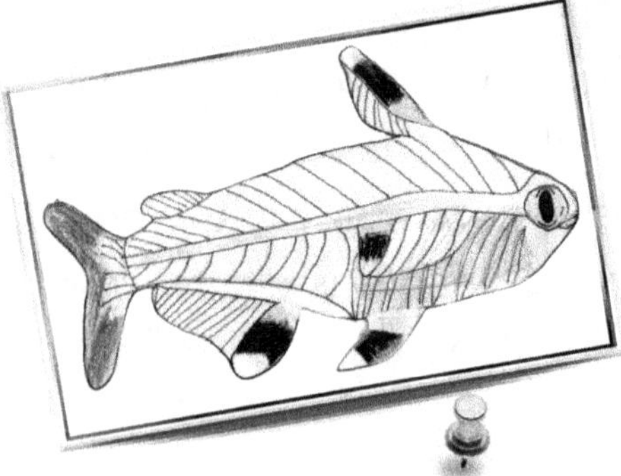

Tell me about my babies.

How do I look?

What do you like best about me?

What do I eat?

COLOR THE WORLD

X5

We have already learned about imaginary lines around the globe that we use to find our way around or locate specific places. If the Animals had had a way to control exactly where they were going, traveling would have been much easier. There are also other markings on the globe that help us be specific with location.

Here are some more markings on the globe:

Latitude–flat lines around the globe

Longitude–long lines around the globe

Degrees–measurements in numbers (the equator is 0 degrees–0° latitude)

Prime Meridian–a 0° longitude line that divides the globe in half; making one side the Western Hemisphere and the other side the Eastern Hemisphere

Northern Hemisphere–the half of the earth that is north of the equator

Southern Hemisphere–the half of the earth that is south of the equator

➡ **It's time to color the world!**
Color the globe markings as follows:
Latitude Lines—GREEN
Longitude Lines—BLUE
Equator—RED (write 0° somewhere on the line)
Prime Meridian—PURPLE (write 0° somewhere on the line)
Northern Hemisphere—YELLOW
Southern Hemisphere—ORANGE

NORTH ATLANTIC

MAP IT!

Barend the Bear remembered some of the places he and Amber the Ant had traveled through during their journeys. Color those places listed below.

1. Color Greenland GREEN.

2. Color Iceland ORANGE.

3. Color Davis Strait BLUE.

4. Color Denmark Strait PURPLE.

X6

YANNI THE YAK

WHAT TIME IS IT, YANNI?

Knowing the time of the day is important, and it has been that way for people all over the world and throughout history. The ancient Egyptians used a sundial, and the Greeks used a water clock. The first mechanical clock was made in AD 723 by a monk and mathematician. A clock is a mechanical or electrical device for measuring time. One of the first records of a clock worn on a person was when Queen Elizabeth received a wristwatch with diamonds as a gift in 1571. She also had a watch set in a ring. The Animals never imagined they would travel the world with the help of a piece of the Ten Commandments tablets. After some wild adventures and a few close calls, they realized they needed a way to control when and where they traveled. And since they were traveling through time, what better device than a clock?

Fill in the empty spaces on the clock above with the correct numbers.

Extra challenge: See if you can count all the clocks in your home, and write the answer here _____.

YAKS

To become a master researcher like Yanni, you must first learn your yak facts. These relatives of cows mostly live in Asia, and some live high up in the mountains. They have long hair and big horns. Boy yaks are usually larger than girls.

All yaks have a layer of long thick wool, which keeps them warm in the snowy mountains. They look like walking mops! However, these mops have special talents that help them high up in the mountains.

Yaks can breathe in a lot of air at once. This is good, because there is not much air that high up. They are herbivores and eat grasses and shrubs. They have more than one stomach, which helps them get as much energy as possible out of the food they eat. They can also swim in freezing waters. Yaks like living up high in the cold so much that if they come down, they could get sick from getting too hot!

Mommy and baby yaks usually form groups called herds, and they stick together. Momma yaks like to be alone to have their babies, but then they go back to the herd very soon, because the baby can stand up after only ten minutes! The babies then grow up to be big and tough to survive in the freezing cold.

When you think of cold weather, what comes to mind? Snowflakes? Icicles? Christmas trees and fuzzy sweaters? Draw a yak in their favorite chilly climate, adding your own wintery festive touch.

YAKS

Y4

In what type of place do I like to live?

How do I look? Describe me.

What do you like best about me?

What do I eat?

CAUGHT IN AN OASIS

We know that there is a lot of water on the surface of the earth. More than half of the surface is water is oceans, rivers, and lakes. We have also learned that there is water in the air. But did you know that there is water *under* the surface of the earth?

Even very dry deserts that stretch on for many miles have water below the sand, and sometimes that water comes to the surface. When you see water surrounded by a desert, it is called an oasis.

Plants and animals are happy to have water to drink in a desert! Except if they get tangled up in the plants, like Yanni the Yak did, of course.

Color the underground current of water BLUE. Make sure to include the water that is flowing up to the surface, where Yanni the Yak is stuck. Then color the sand above the water YELLOW or TAN.

OCEANS

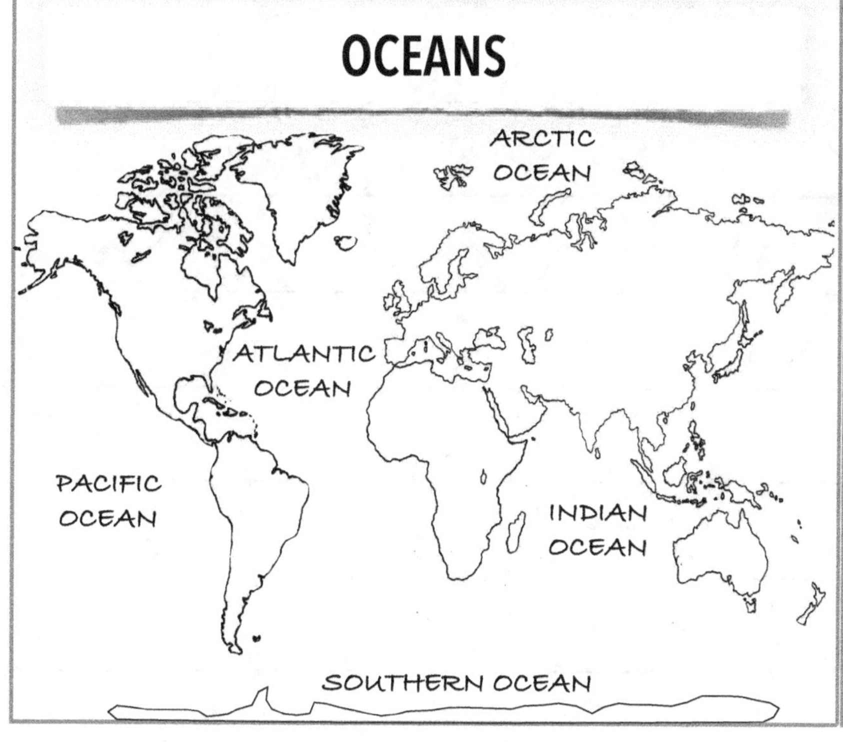

MAP IT!

Traveling over the five oceans was no problem for the Animals, with the help of the Commandment Stone. Color the oceans listed below.

1. Color the Pacific Ocean BLUE.

2. Color the Atlantic Ocean GREEN.

3. Color the Indian Ocean YELLOW.

4. Color the Arctic Ocean PINK.

5. Color the Southern Ocean PURPLE.

Y6

ZERLOCK THE ZEBRA

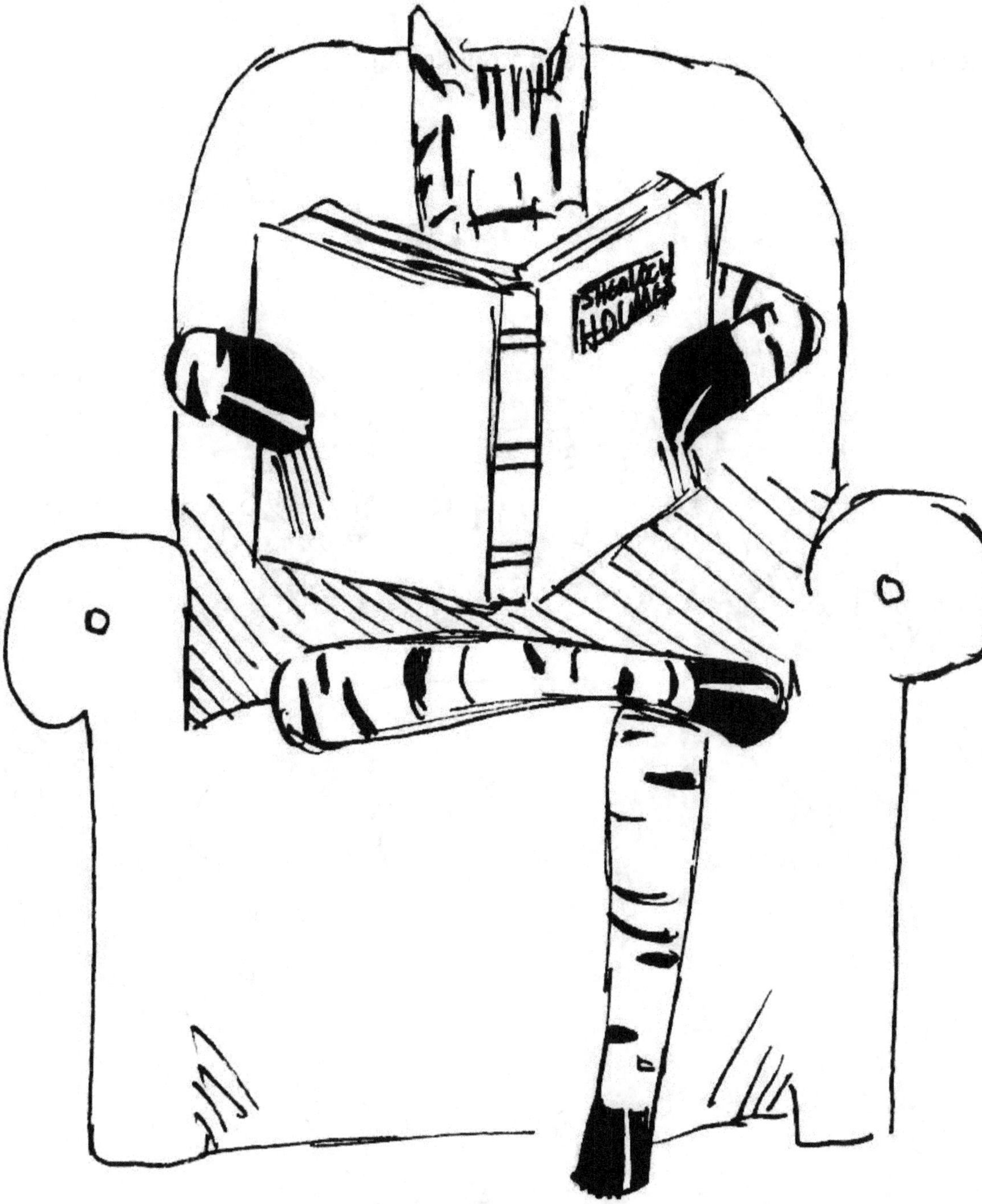

FIND EACH FREEDOM SEEKER

The Animals traveled through time and space, seeing moments in history they would never forget. They saw the clothing and customs of different cultures. Some ate the food and listened to the music of different peoples. They even saw battles fought over the topic of freedom. It was only when they met Zerlock the Zebra, however, that they were challenged to seek the true meaning of freedom—they were now FREEDOM SEEKERS!

Color the Animals as you make sure they are all accounted for.

ZEBRAS

Zebras are very interesting creatures with beautiful black and white stripe patterns on their bodies. You can get dizzy if you look at one too long! They might look like horses, but they have very special talents that help them in their natural homes.

Zebras use their stripes to blend into the tall grasses in their home. This helps them hide from hunters like lions who would like to catch them. Because they are related to horses and donkeys, zebras sleep standing up. Again, this gives them extra time to run away if something comes after them.

Can your ears move all by themselves? If you think that's special, you'll love what a zebra can do! They use their ears to tell others if they're happy, or scared, or sleepy. They have extra-long tails, too, to brush away flies and other pests. They like to eat grass, but lots of other animals like to eat zebras! If something chases them, zebras dash from side to side, confusing the predator and making themselves harder to chase.

Even though zebras have many amazing talents, like great sight and hearing, they are most famous for their stripes. People even named street crosswalks zebra crossings, because of the black and white stripes. Look out when the zebra crosses!

Fill this box with your own unique zebra pattern of stripes. You can also choose a unique color for your stripes.

ZEBRAS

Z4

How do I use my ears?

What do I eat?

What do you like best about me?

What am I scared of? What do I do to protect myself?

NO ORDINARY STONE

Stones come in all shapes, sizes, colors, and textures. Some are ordinary stones you kick around when taking a walk, but others are considered precious stones and they are so valuable they are kept locked in safes. Diamonds are a type of stone made from the same material as the lead in your pencil—carbon. But the carbon that makes a diamond goes through a special process to become so precious. When carbon far below the earth's surface is under immense heat and pressure, the look and structure change, and a diamond develops. Did you know that diamonds come in all different colors? Some are white, blue, yellow, orange, red, green, pink, and purple.

The Animals don't know much about the Commandment Stone, but they know it's not an ordinary stone to be kicked around. Color the stone in any color or combination of colors that YOU like.

CONTINENTS

MAP IT!

Traveling over the seven continents was no problem for the Animals, with the help of the Commandment Stone. Color the continents listed below.

1. Color North America RED.

2. Color South America ORANGE.

3. Color Africa YELLOW.

4. Color Europe GREEN.

5. Color Asia BLUE.

6. Color Australia PURPLE.

7. Color Antarctica PINK.